As the finger[...]round
the Clock' fi[...]y and
Johnny bopp[...]

'So how're m[...]nands
on her should[...] gesture.

Chills ran down Penny's spine.

'Not bad!' she lied, trying to conceal her trembling chin.

'Not bad!'

His hand slid down and tightened around her waist, pulling her toward him, almost throwing her off balance. She started to laugh. Johnny did too. He moved toward her, sliding his fingers sensuously over her bare arms and touching her trembling lips with his fingers. His fingers were cool and smooth as they touched her and Penny tingled.

'No, Johnny, don't,' she protested meekly . . .

Also available and published by Bantam Books:

BABY, IT'S YOU
HELLO, STRANGER
SAVE THE LAST DANCE FOR ME
BREAKING UP IS HARD TO DO
OUR DAY WILL COME

Stand By Me

N.H. KLEINBAUM

STAND BY ME
A BANTAM BOOK   0 553 40122 X
Originally published in Great Britain by Bantam Books

PRINTING HISTORY
Bantam edition published 1990

TM and © MCMLXXXVII Vestron Pictures Inc.

Text copyright © 1990 by Transworld Publishers Ltd.

This book is set in 11 on 13 Palatino

Bantam Books are published by Transworld Publishers Ltd., 61–63
Uxbridge Road, Ealing, London W5 5SA, in Australia by Transworld
Publishers (Australia) Pty. Ltd., 15–23 Helles Avenue, Moorebank,
NSW 2170, and in New Zealand by Transworld Publishers (N.Z.)
Ltd., Cnr. Moselle and Waipareira Avenues, Henderson, Auckland.

Made and printed in Great Britain by
Cox & Wyman Ltd, Reading, Berks.

STAND BY ME

One

Frances Kellerman smiled as she delivered plates of eggs, toast and bacon. She estimated that so far during her five weeks of waitressing this summer at Kellerman's Hotel in the Catskill Mountains of New York State she must have carried ten thousand plates of food.

As she shuttled her tray of dirty dishes back into the kitchen, she noticed Norman the bellhop wolfing down some of Gino the chef's fresh hot danish.

Norman's job was to schlepp bags for guests; he also practised his comedy routine on the new-arrivals so that their vacation started off with a laugh.

As she looked around the kitchen, Neil Mumford was pouring himself a glass of orange juice. Frances heard the chief cook shouting at Neil to get back to the pool.

'My job is a piece of cake,' he often boasted to the waiters, who sweated as they carried heavy trays of hot dishes back and forth three meals a day.

Frances shook her head in disgust as she thought of how Neil's eyes always followed the sexy bodies in skimpy bikinis walking around the pool. When he wasn't girl-watching, Neil concentrated on making sure his tan was perfectly even.

'This kitchen is really hopping today,' she thought as she moved quickly to pick up her order. Her cousin, Robin Kellerman, bustled in, nibbling on an English muffin.

'Hi, Baby,' Robin smiled, calling her by the familiar and commonly-used nickname Frances had since early childhood. 'This muffin's cold,' she complained. 'Any hot muffins?' she asked as she looked around for something even more caloric to nibble.

Unable to find the muffins, she persisted. 'Gino, any more little cheese danish?' she asked the chef.

'Didn't you already have breakfast?' Baby asked, smiling at her loveable, but slightly chubby cousin.

'Yeah, but that was at least an hour ago! I just need a little nosh . . . a little something,' she smiled wanly.

Robin's idea of working for the summer was polishing her toenails without smudging one, or ironing her hair and not having the humidity frizz it up again.

Frances didn't have much time to ponder how things had changed so quickly, since this morning,

as usual, the guests were clamoring for more food.
She picked up her order and went back to ask who
wanted seconds.

As she walked toward her station, Frances
noticed Johnny Castle and Penny Lopez eating at
the back of the dining room. The pair led dance
classes, and performed on stage on Saturday
nights, sometimes with big-name show stoppers
like Bobby Darin. Sometimes they performed their
own interpretations of mambos and cha-cha-chas
to receptive audiences, all of whom dreamed they
could move, glide and slide with the grace of the
handsome dancing instructors.

Everyone always managed to make their time
at Kellerman's a vacation, whether they were
working or visiting, Frances thought happily.

She'd never really liked the idea of her father
taking over the hotel from her Uncle Jake. Somewhere in the back of her mind she connected it to
her parent's divorce. The hotel had been a place
for him to run to, and the home where she and
her older sister Lisa had grown up in Roslyn, Long
Island, was the place he had run from. But that
was behind them all now. And since she'd been
working at the hotel she felt a certain amount of
pride in it.

'You won't get a chance to do this tomorrow
when you're home and the vacation is over!' the
buoyant Max Kellerman, would always remind
reluctant guests. After a lecture from Max they
would nod in agreement and end up joining the

activities, whether it was Simon Sez or a limbo dancing contest.

Baby smiled at her father who was patting guests on the shoulders. He smiled at her weakly.

In truth, Max was giving an Academy Award performance, keeping up his usual cheerful demeanor. Behind the scenes, things were rotten at Kellerman's and Max was scared. He vowed never to confide his problems to his daughter but he finally had to face reality when the bottom fell out.

On a cloudy day in early August, Max sat hunched over an adding machine, the rhythmic clicking stopping and starting as his fingers played over the tiny keyboard.

He sat behind his desk hour after hour, sheets of paper spread everywhere, a long tape curling out of the adding machine.

Finally, the clicking stopped.

Max put his head in his hands on the desk, surrounded by a blizzard of paper, and wept. Shaking his head, he took a deep breath. 'I just don't get it. My father made this place work. My brother Jake made it work. Why can't I make *anything* work!'

'My insurance job was a dead end, my marriage ended in divorce. This was going to be it . . . the answer to my prayers. And now everything is falling apart at once!'

He continued his computations, overwhelmed by self-pity, sighing and moaning as the numbers kept coming up in the red when Sweets, his long-time friend and piano player strolled in the door.

Sweets looked around at the stacks and piles of papers and adding machine tapes, raised his eyebrows and whistled.

'Looks like you got some mess in here, buddy,' Sweets said, sliding into a swivel chair and sitting opposite Max.

Max didn't answer. He blew his nose into a big plaid handkerchief, making a loud honking sound that made Sweets jump in spite of himself. Then Max started to tabulate on the adding machine again.

Sweets sat watching quietly for a few minutes.

'I'm hearin' a buzz, boss,' he said, finally breaking the silence.

'Did you have your ears checked?' Max asked, not looking up from his columns of figures.

'No, man, it's not my ears.'

'Must be the adding machine,' Max said, pretending to concentrate on the machine.

Sweets shook his head. 'Uh–uh. Not that kinda buzz, Maxy. Rumors. Bad rumors. Chef says the butcher wants a check for the meat, not a free golf lesson.

'Word is you're not restocking the bar. And the kids . . .'

Max looked up. 'What did they say?'

Sweets leaned on the table. Sweat poured down Max's forehead. His eyes were moist. Sweets saw the pain and the truth in his friend's red eyes.

'Feel like talkin'?' Sweets asked quietly.

Max sighed, scanning the papers, throwing up his hands in dispair.

'What? What did they say?' he repeated, looking up, pale and drawn, from amidst the sheaves of messy papers.

Max sighed, and gazed down helplessly at the piles of colored receipts, overdue bill notices, bank statements and bounced check reports.

'I don't know what to do,' Max wailed. 'The rain July fourth killed us. We needed new roofing – we roofed. I had to replaster the pool . . . were people supposed to swim in their bathtubs? That's what they come here for! Reseeding the lawn . . . new awnings . . . maintenance and more maintenance and all at once! All of a sudden! Now I'm ten grand in the hole and all of Sullivan County, not to mention the employees and their families, are yelling down my back.'

Sweets shook his head. 'Bad scene, Max, bad scene. But I don't think it helped that you let that leggy redhead do your books. What happened to Irwin after all these years? He always kept things in balance.'

'Irwin? Irwin got tired. Burned out. Told me so himself. He and the wife wanted out. He went to live near his daughter in Phoenix. How do you find someone like Irwin to trust?' Max asked painfully, giving Sweets a look for the redhead remark. 'Juanita was good with figures,' Max said. 'She told me so herself.'

Sweets let out a hoot of laughter! 'Oh she did, did she? Good with figures? I think the only figures that broad was good with were 36-24-36 and you fell right in the trap, Max. What *are* we going to do with you! Good with figures, my ass,' Sweets - chuckled.

'If you weren't in such a mess and if I didn't love you like a brother I'd probably laugh myself all the way over to the bar and repeat that whole stupid story,'

'But this stuff is business. Serious business and we got to figure out something to do.'

'I know,' Max sighed. 'Know any millionaires who owe you a favor?'

Sweets laughed. 'Believe me Max, if I did, you know I'd grovel to get it for you. But there must be another way. It's only money. You're in good health, the place still has life in it, we'll find the answer. It will probably be where we least expect it.'

Max smiled. 'I guess you're right, Sweets. You usually are.'

Sweets chuckled. 'What a team we are, huh, boss?'

There was a knock on the door and a middle-aged man wearing a grimy denim plumber's uniform walked in, adding up a row of figures on a dirty notepad as Max and Sweets eyed him.

'So, Mr Rothman?' Max said. 'Did you bring me good news or money? That I could use. Anything else . . .'

'Well,' Rothman said, ignoring the remark and still figuring on the notepad, as he moistened the tip of the lead pencil in his mouth every few minutes.

'Well,' he repeated triumphantly, 'I found the problem. Rothman always finds the problem for you, right Max? The problem is . . . your main boiler's shot. Kaput. Gonzo. You're lucky you have any water at all.'

Max's face fell.

'How much?'

'OK,' Rothman said, in his mathematical glory, 'Now we get down to the nitty-gritty. I got your regular estimate and I got your discount estimate. Figure I'd give you a choice. 'Course, with the discount, you gotta provide your own adhesive tape and paper clips to hold her together!'

Rothman laughed hysterically, tears coming into his eyes, as Max grew red in the face.

'What're you, auditioning for the Saturday night show here as a comedian, or giving me a plumbing estimate? Forget the adhesive tape. This is Kellerman's! We have a reputation to uphold! What're you telling me?'

'You need a new unit. Not today, Max. Not tomorrow. Yesterday,' Rothman said, stifling a chuckle.

'I got that, Mr Comedian. Now give me the punchline.'

'This part, you might not think so funny,' Rothman said, getting down to numbers and business. He figured on his notepad as the color drained from Max's face. Sweets sat silently, watching his boss's painful suffering.

'You got the boiler itself, plus all our hotwater lines, installation . . . that comes to eight thousand, two hundred fifty-six dollars and seventy cents . . . give or take . . .'

Max paled even further.

'What if I install it myself?' he asked, appalled at the cost, which would only add to his burden, 'Does it come with a book or anything?'

'A book?' Rothman laughed. 'Maxy, that's a good one, a book. The book we study in plumbing school, sure, but that's not for learning on the job at a big hotel like this. Look, your people could all take cold showers, it's good for the circulation and other things.' He winked at Sweets.

'Max,' Rothman continued, 'the boiler's in. desperate shape. As a friend, I'll get my men on it right away if you want me to, before it blows and you're really in hot water! Hot water!' he screamed. 'I'm funnier than even I thought!'

Max looked ill.

'I'll call you in the morning,' Max said, as Rothman headed toward the door. 'It will last that long, won't it?'

'From your mouth to God's ears!' Rothman winked as he slammed the door shut on Max and Sweets.

'This is it, Sweets,' Max sighed. 'To think that water would end up drowning Kellerman's! We swim in water, we boat and sail in water. My father bought this land because of the beautiful lake. Water! Now I can't afford the money to give these people hot water to clean themselves, let alone for cooking and everything else.'

'Have faith, Max,' Sweets sighed, as he stood and patted his buddy on the back, 'I have a feeling something good will come from all this bad. Funny, but that has a way of happening, whether it's water or broads!'

He winked and walked out the door.

Two

'Okay,' Johnny called, 'let's give this conga a chance one more time. Now hold on to the waist or shoulders of the person in front of you, depending which you can reach, or which you'd like to grab.' Everybody laughed as the odd assortment of bodies smiled at each other.

'Now,' Johnny called, 'ready, go!'

Penny put the needle on the record player and hopped in line behind Johnny as the music began.

'One–two–three–four, con-ga,' he called, 'one–two–three–four–con-ga!' The class, weaved around the room, circling tables and chairs with Johnny playfully calling out the beat until the music stopped.

'Great lesson, folks!' Johnny complimented, as the guests conga-ed out the door! 'See you tomorrow at ten! This time we'll meet at the pool, weather permitting, so we can show off all we've learned!'

The older ladies giggled and poked one another

at the thought, as they counted and bumped, doing the Latin dance with a movement probably never seen south of the border.

Johnny turned off the record. 'I'm beat!' he sighed, slumping into a chair as Penny continued to conga around, full of energy.

'What did *you* eat for breakfast?' he asked.

'Whatever it was, you ought to try some. You're a real party-pooper and we have another class in fifteen minutes!' she jibbed.

Johnny moaned.

'I'm tired. I don't know why. I just need a vacation.'

'This *is* a vacation, dear boy,' she smiled. 'Remember? Just think back to working with your dad and brother in the garage. Doing the conga with a bunch of out of shape old biddies beats that or my bagging groceries in the supermarket as far as I'm concerned!'

'You're right,' Johnny said, suddenly brightening. 'I guess it just hit me this morning that the summer is half over. Before we know it, like it or not, we *will* be going back to that reality. Bobby Darin liked our dance for his big show warm-up at Kellerman's last month, but, as usual, it didn't take us anywhere!'

'Hey, where's the spirit! The dream! The hope you told me you talked to your Dad about! Come on, Johnny, this is our hope and we got to keep with it. Never give up. Until our legs do, anyhow.'

'Legs like yours will never give up, Penny, even when you're ninety. The guys in the old age home will be fighting over you!'

'Enough!' she shouted. 'I don't want to think or talk about old age homes. I love the conga and I want to do it. Come on, up on your feet, tired boy. Let's make the most of being here, now, while we can forget about Jersey and the life we left behind . . . at least for a little while.'

She put on the music again, the beat filling the air, her contagious rhythm catching hold of Johnny who grabbed her and started to dance.

He wrapped his arms tightly around her tiny waist.

'What is this, a new move?' she asked.

Johnny pulled back, hurt and surprised. 'You don't like it?'

'It's not the conga!' she laughed.

'What is it?'

'You know, you think you're so hot, such a great dancer. The ladies all swoon no matter what you do with those slinky hips, but *you* really can't conga. I was watching you.'

His mouth twisted wryly. 'I can't conga! Are you crazy! It's one of my specialties!'

Penny grabbed hold of him, taking the role of the teacher with Johnny now the student.

'It's the hips,' she explained seriously. 'You don't have enough Cuban rhythm in your hips.'

Johnny looked askance. 'What are you talking about?' he asked, pushing away.

Penny shrugged her shoulders.

'You don't. I do. I have Cuban rhythm!'

'You got a head start, *chica*, remember that!' he laughed.

'OK, you got me there,' she smiled, 'but you *can* learn it. It's just the rhythm. You gotta give more on the push. Like this. Da-da-da-*da-da*!'

'That's what I'm doing!' Johnny protested. '*Da-da*.'

Penny shook her head. 'No. You're doin' da-da-da-*da-da-da*.'

'That's what I did! That's the right way.'

Penny shook her head again. 'Put your hands on my hips. Do what I do . . .'

Johnny put his hands on her hips, following her.

'You feel that? You feel that thing in my hips?' she asked seriously.

Johnny smiled mischievously. 'Whatever it is, I like it . . .'

'OK, now,' Penny said rolling her eyes, 'now give me a little more *umph*.'

'I'm giving it *umph*! What do you want from . . . ?'

The lesson was interrupted as Tammy, one of the dancers, came running breathlessly into the ballroom.

'They're in here guys,' she called behind her, as she ran toward Johnny, followed by three other dancers, Rita, Eddie and Rocco.

'What's up?' Penny asked, as she took the needle off the record player. The huge ballroom suddenly echoed as they all started to shout and explain at once.

'Hold it, hold it,' Johnny said. 'Let's sit down a minute. My ankle still hurts every so often from that twist I took. Sit down and let's talk one at a time.'

Tammy started. 'We still haven't got our pay checks this week and it's Thursday!'

Johnny shrugged, unconcerned. 'So go talk to the man. By now we know we can talk to him. He likes us. He likes our dancing. There must be some screw-up or something.'

'We talked to him,' Eddie said.

'Yeah, he said stuff like, "Not now Rocco, I gotta go to ping-pong finals." '

Rita, a petite brunette, stood up. 'The point is, he's avoiding us, Johnny. Something's up. This never happened before and he never put us off like this before. He's acting funny too, I think,' she observed. 'Sometimes, I see him just staring off into space, like he's not really here. Or wishes he weren't.'

'Nothing's up,' Johnny reassured them. 'Believe me . . . there are two things you can depend on the old guy for . . . bugging you and paying you. The rest is unpredictable. One day he loves you, the next day he's having one of those hormone attacks. Forget it, we'll get the paychecks. Max is good to his word. He learned to trust me and I've learned to trust him.'

Johnny headed toward the record player and put the conga music back on.

He took Penny's hand and led her to the middle of the floor. She stood in front of him and he put his arms happily back around her waist.

'What do you expect?' Eddie shrugged, getting up and walking to the door with Rocco. 'He's gonna listen to us when he's dancing?'

'I listened,' Johnny yelled over the beat, as he followed Penny. 'Come on, you wanna conga with us? You just gotta follow Miss Expert here . . . It's on the da-da-*da*.'

'*Da-da*!' Penny added. 'I told you, you need the extra *da-da*!'

Eddie laughed. 'You two enjoy yourselves. We gotta go to work.'

'What do you think *we're* doin'?' Johnny shouted over the music, as the other kids walked out laughing, momentarily appeased by Johnny. Johnny and Penny danced with electricity to the beat of the Cuban music.

The record ended.

'Better, much better,' Penny lightly clapped her hands as she took the record off the machine.

'Better?' Johnny said, smiling benignly. 'It was perfect.'

'Not yet,' Penny said, shaking her hips. 'I'll tell you when it's perfect. You know I always do.' She gave him a sexy wink.

Penny slipped the record into the cardboard folder and pursed her lips.

'Do you think there could be anything to what they say?' she asked Johnny. 'Now that I think about it, Max did look awfully worried today. Even when he's schmoozing around with the guests he has this glazed-over look in his eyes, as though he's there, like Rita said, but . . . but he's not really there. Sort of like going through the motions.'

Johnny shook his head. 'Nah!' He, too, had noticed Max's preoccupation, his sudden temper and heightened anxiety. But he didn't want to worry Penny. And, he admitted to himself, he didn't really want to believe that anything was wrong.

Besides, he thought, Baby would have said something to him if there were problems. They had developed a special relationship. One like he'd never quite had before. He couldn't even describe it.

No denying he was attracted to her. But she was college stuff, out of his league. He didn't even want to think of her as a summer romance. She was a special friend, that was it, he decided. Romance he had had with Penny and with Delia, his first love and his first dancing teacher.

But with Baby it was different. If Max did have problems, Baby would need to talk to Johnny as much as he would need to talk to her about things. That's the way it had developed after their first fiery encounter.

He taught her to dance, to loosen up, and she loved it. She taught him to loosen up, too, only in a different, more personal way. Nothing physical. It was sharing your thoughts and feelings. The kind of thing he could never do at home. Never even do with Penny, as much as he cared for her in another different way.

'Say, are you tuning out like Max or what?' Penny asked, interrupting Johnny's reverie.

'Oh no, I was just thinking about that gorgeous bookkeeper he got when Irwin left. Max is probably still mooning over her sudden departure. You know the old lover boy. Can't keep him away from the pretty ladies.'

'Yeah,' Penny said, thinking to herself, as they walked together out of the ballroom. 'But she *did* leave suddenly. And things have been different since then. That's when Max started being late with the checks. You don't think . . .' She looked at Johnny.

'Nah! She probably just screwed up the paper-work and it's taking him a while to straighten it out. Besides, it's hard to find someone to pick up the pieces here in the boonies of upstate New York in the middle of the summer. Max will be fine. He's a tough guy.' Johnny took Penny's hand and squeezed it hard.

'You're right,' she smiled, as they walked toward the pool for the outdoor mambo lesson next on the day's activities.

Three

'You ever hear of a resort getting by without hot water?' Max asked Sweets who swiveled in the chair opposite the dour-faced owner, beside himself over his seemingly insurmountable problems.

'How about meat?' Max continued. 'How about a staff?'

Sweets swiveled and took a deep breath, poking on his upper molar with a toothpick.

'I think you gotta rob Peter to pay Paul,' he said. 'And this meat, really is getting bad,' he added, poking at his tooth.

'Great! Now I'm getting Bible lessons, as well as complaints! Sweets, I'm at the end of my rope here. If it's pulled a little tighter, my neck will be gone!'

Sweets cleared his throat as a signal to Max when he spotted Baby at the door.

'Dad,' Baby said, walking in boldly without a greeting to either of her two favorite people, 'the kids're talking about not getting—'

'Paid. I know, Baby, I know.'

'So?'

'So . . . I'm afraid it's true, honey.' Max paused and gulped. 'I'm broke. Between the repairs and the upkeep and that miserable fourth of July that kept droves of people away, it's just not there. I was playing this game close to the edge to begin with,' he admitted, 'but now I'm over the edge. Things look real bad.'

Baby reached over to her father and out her arms around his neck. 'Oh, Dad . . . I'm sorry. Are you OK? Is there anything I can do?'

'Well, the truth is, I'm not OK,' he sighed. 'But I'll live.'

'What're we going to do?' Baby asked, sitting down next to Sweets, who squeezed her hand.

'I don't think I have many choices,' Max sighed. 'I don't want to lose the hotel. I think I'm going to have to let some people—'

'No!' Baby nearly shouted, jumping up and interrupting her father. 'Not the staff. There's *got* to be some other way.'

'What?' Max asked as his mouth dipped into an even deeper frown.

'Look,' Baby said, 'I don't need a salary. Don't pay me.'

'That's very sweet, honey,' her father smiled sadly. 'But I wasn't very generous to you in the first place. You mostly work on tips. It wouldn't come close to solving the problem.'

'I know, Dad, but it's a start,' Baby said, getting excited and feeling a bit more hopeful. 'Look, it's the middle of the summer already. If we let people go now, they're going to have a hard time getting other work.

'They depend on this money. Lots of them send most of it home. For some, it's more than they make all winter long. Oh, we can't let the staff go!' she cried.

'You think I don't know all that!' Max answered angrily.

Baby sat quietly.

'There's *got* to be a way,' Baby said in a rush of emotion. 'We cannot let Kellerman's go down the tubes, not after all the years, the history, the effort that went into making it an institution! People automatically think Kellerman's when they think of coming to the Catskills. Grandpa and Uncle Jake worked too hard, not to mention what you've done, to work to save the hotel.'

'Listen, I'm a whiz at math. Maybe it's just a question of figuring out where the problem is and then we'll solve it. I'll get someone to take my waitressing station and work on this full time. Then we can sit down together and figure out . . . something. Dad, I *know* there's a solution . . . there has to be!'

'Honey . . .' Max started, a beaten man, humiliated and frustrated in front of his own child. 'OK, look things over, if it'll make you feel better. Give it a shot. You always did get good grades in math.'

'Dad, I got good grades in everything, remember?' she smiled, as she raced out the door, her face filled with determination.

'Good luck kid,' he called, as she was already down the hallway. 'And thanks.'

Max looked at Sweets. 'She's almost like a son to me,' he sighed.

'A son! Max, you're my friend, like a brother, man, but you're a jerk. She's better than a son! You might have a son who said, "Tough luck, Charlie. Just 'cause you can't run a business don't look to me for help." There's plenty of sons out there like that.

'But not Baby. She's a lady and a smart woman, who's never been afraid to work and never been afraid to do and say the right thing. You couldn't be prouder of her no matter what she was. If I had a kid, I'd want *her* to be just like Baby.'

A tear dripped slowly down Max's face. 'You're right, Sweets. She's some special kid. I am lucky to have her.'

'Anyway.' Sweets said, trying to lighten the mood, 'you know what they say about sons. They're yours till they find them a wife, but a daughter's a daughter the rest of your life! That Baby is no baby, Max. She's some special woman. I hope she finds a guy good enough for her, not like that lifeguard you were trying to push at her.'

'That guy's gonna be a doctor, Sweets!'

'Lots of jerky doctors out there, Max. He doesn't have the heart and soul Baby needs. Neil just thinks about Neil.'

Max considered this. 'Maybe you're right. You know, Sweets, you're my own private philosopher. 'I don't know what I'd do without you!'

'Well, if you don't start paying me soon, you might have to find out!' Sweets laughed.

Max's face darkened.

'Hey, brother,' said Sweets. 'That was a joke. 'I'm here for bread or no bread. You can always count on Sweets!'

Max stood up and reached out toward Sweets. He hugged him, saying what words could not express.

Sweets cleared his throat, obviously moved by the emotion. 'Yea, well, listen, now, you got a lot of other kids out there wonderin' what's goin' down. You owe 'em . . . something, Max.'

Max nodded and moaned. 'Oh God, where are those antacids?'

Four

Baby bolted from her father's office in the main house to the poolside where she knew she'd find Robin.

She saw her from the distance, covered with sun tan oil, holding a reflector to her face, bulging out of her supposedly slimming tanksuit.

Baby walked up to Robin with dazzling determination, balancing a tray, which she set down on Robin's knees.

'What's this? I didn't order anything.' Robin said, looking suspiciously at the empty tray and Baby's hard-set face. 'Although,' she smiled, 'it is getting humid, waitress, and a lemonade on the rocks with a cherry would be nice.'

'Get up, Robin,' Baby ordered.

Robin sat up, blinking with bafflement.

'Why?'

'You're about to have a life experience – one you probably never even dreamed of in your wildest fantasies.'

'Robin swung her legs around and stood up, excited.

'Is it a guy? It's a guy, right? I just know it's a guy. Steve? Where is he? He has a surprise for me? He told you something wonderful about me? Tell me, the suspense is killing me,' Robin begged.

'Sorry, Robin,' Baby said, as she folded her cousin's big pool towel and started to put her cousin's sun lotion, oils, Noxzema and zinc oxide in her multi-colored beach bag. 'It's not Steve. But, in a way, it could help Steve. And a lot of others too. In fact, you could be a heroine, Robin. You could be the heroine of this wonderful life experience fantasy.'

'What?' Robin asked, running after Baby who had taken her pool things and was heading toward the main building.

Baby turned and faced Robin head on.

'OK, cuz, here it is. We're in trouble. Big money trouble. My father needs as much free help as he can get or else he'll have to fire some of the staff. Maybe even Steve. I need you to take my shift so I can try and figure out what kind of mess his latest flame, the bookkeeper, made out of the place that *our* grandfather founded. *Comprendez*? Robin, I need your help!'

Robin turned. 'You're in my sun,' she said, ignoring Baby's pleading eyes.

'Robin . . .'

'You seriously want *me* to wait tables?' Robin asked. '*Me*? I don't know the first thing about . . .'

'It's very simple,' Baby said, hoping she had finally struck the right chord and had Robin on her side. 'Rule number 1 – the customer is always right. If the soup is cold, get another one. If the meat's not done enough, bring it back to be cooked more. but make sure you know which piece it is and return the same one because we're short on meat!'

Robin looked at Baby in disbelief.

'Rule number one is the customer is always right, huh?' Robin shouted. 'Well, I'm the customer and I don't want to do it. Therefore, I'm right!'

'You're wrong!' Baby said. 'You're a Kellerman. Your father ran this place before mine. Your history is here just as much as mine. Your responsibility to keep our family name good is just as important, just as real, as mine. So, Miss Customer, you're wrong, because you're not a customer, you're family!'

'But, I'm only seventeen! You're talking about child labor . . .' Robin rambled.

'I'm talking survival, Robin. I'm talking teamwork and family.'

Baby looked at her cousin, whose lip began to quiver.

'I never did this before. I never did anything. What if I drop a tray or spill something?'

'Someone will always be nearby, I promise,' Baby said, crossing her fingers behind her back. 'Are you a Kellerman, Robin, or not?' she asked, going for the jugular.

'OK,' Robin said reluctantly. 'But if this is going to ruin my nails . . .'

Baby hugged Robin for an instant and handed her the tray.

'Now, hurry, go get a uniform from Mary in central supply. Then shower off that gook you've got on you and take this tray to the main dining room. Look for Steve and tell him you're covering for me. Don't tell him why, though. Just ask him to give you a quick lesson in what to do.'

Robin looked aghast.

'Are you kidding?'

'We're past jokes, Robin. Ask Steve. You know he'll help you. Now, do it. And hurry!'

Baby raced back to the main house with Robin watching in bewilderment.

'What *have* I got myself into?' Robin thought, as she picked up the tray and practised holding it waitress-style as she walked to central supply.

'Not bad,' she said, as she saw her reflection in a glass door. 'By George, I'll do it!'

Five

As the finger-snapping rhythm of Bill Haley's 'Rock Around the Clock' filled the ballroom rehearsal hall, Penny and Johnny bopped to the music.

'So how're my hips now?' Johnny asked as he put his hands on her shoulders in a sexy, possessive gesture.

Chills ran down Penny's spine.

'Not bad!' she lied, trying to conceal her trembling chin.

'Not bad!'

His hand slid down and tightened around her waist, pulling her toward him, almost throwing her off balance. She started to laugh. Johnny did too. He moved toward her, sliding his fingers sensuously over her bare arms and touching her trembling lips with his fingers. His fingers were cool and smooth as they touched her and Penny tingled.

'No, Johnny, don't,' she protested meekly.

He tenderly traced the line of her cheekbone and jaw, smiling his irresistibly devastating grin.

'What a gorgeous smile!' she thought.

Suddenly, their faces were very close together and before either of them knew what had happened, they kissed, deeply, neither willing nor able to pull back.

'God, I'm sorry,' he said, as his gaze traveled over her face and searched her eyes.

'Me, too,' Penny smiled, her heart jolted, her pulse pounding.

'Wow . . .'

'Yeah.'

They stood silently, both feeling an almost unwelcome surge of excitement.

'What are you looking at?' Penny asked.

Johnny scanned her and beamed approval.

'Oh, I don't know,' he lied.

'Come on, Johnny,' Penny said, noticing that he was watching her intently, angry and yet feeling powerless to resist a warm delight.

'You're still doing it,' she said as she saw him look at her with an obvious double meaning.

'It's not good for us,' she continued. 'This would be dangerous. You know it. I know it. This shouldn't have happened.'

The smoldering flame she saw in his eyes both startled and thrilled her, even as she protested.

'I know, I know,' Johnny said, looking away. 'We either dance . . . or . . . but not both.' Penny watched his handsome profile and her heart pounded. There was an intangible bond between them. They'd been friends since they were kids, she reminded herself. It wasn't unnatural that they should feel . . .

'It didn't work before,' Penny reminded him, her heart hammering in her ears.

'I'm not arguing, Pen,' he said. 'It just happened. I saw you and wanted you. Like a magnet I felt drawn to your mouth. I guess the dancing was exciting and all. I'm sorry. You're right. It didn't work before. I'm not arguing.'

'So,' Penny said, aching for his touch, 'We're gonna just dance, right? Just dance.'

'Right!' Johnny said, as he took her in his arms. They both started to dance, fast and furiously, again. The record ended and Penny walked over to take off the needle.

'Pen?' Johnny called. 'How about a slow one, just soft music, for old times sake?'

'Sure,' she smiled, as a tingling raced through her blood. She put a soft tune on the record player and they danced, slowly. He caressed her cheek, smiling sadly.

'It's best, I guess, that we do just dance,' he whispered in her ear.

Penny's heart fluttered as tears welled in her eyes.

'But I want you to know that I'll always care for you. Not the way I've ever loved anyone else or ever will.'

She shook her head as tears trembled on her eyelids. She rested her head on Johnny's shoulder. The music played and they danced, silently pledging to be friends forever.

Penny wiped her eyes and pulled herself together.

'You know,' she said, relieved to change the subject, 'Lester told me he heard that Max really *is* in trouble and might be laying people off. Seems Robin took Baby's waitress station today so she could try and make sense out of the bookkeeping.'

'Robin? Waitressing? This I have to see,' Johnny laughed, but his smile vanished quickly with concern.

'We better look into this,' he admitted. 'I'll ask Baby.'

Penny's heart throbbed at the thought of Johnny and Baby.

'If Max lays people off, we could have deep trouble,' Penny sighed.

Six

Later in the afternoon, Max and Sweets were back in the office, this time looking over a long list of names.

'Max, don't forget,' Sweets said, 'they're not just names, they're people. With families and responsibilities. We can't just throw them out in the street . . .'

'Don't think I've forgotten that, Sweets. I thought you knew me better than that. But what am I to do? Some of these kids will have to go. I simply can't pay them all.'

Sweets sighed.

In a corner, Baby sat silently pouring over a ledger, making notes and checking receipts, as the two men worked on the 'hit list'.

'Rogan, Mark,' Max said, referring to a staff member. 'OK, he gets two points for seniority . . . and then five points against him for that impression he did of me on talent night. I still don't understand why people laughed . . .'

'Because he was funny, man!' Sweets said. 'He

hit you like a nail on the head! Mark's a regular guy. Hard worker. He's a Kellerman man! Besides, boss, this point system, it's jive . . .'

'Well, what else am I supposed to do?' Max said. 'Hold a lottery or something? Ask for volunteers, close my eyes and pick people? I want to be a little more fair than the Spanish Inquisition,' he sighed.

'We're gonna be here till . . .' Sweets started.

'As long as it takes,' Max said, interrupting Sweets. 'OK, next, Fantina, Cherise. One point for seniority. Two points for being cute.'

'Jive, Max! This is just plain jive!'

'OK,' Max conceded. 'One point.'

Meanwhile, Baby sat glued to her seat in the corner, trying to make the numbers work so none of the names her father was mentioning would have to get a pink slip.

'But, Dad, there has to be a way,' Baby begged later that night, as her father looked over the final list, preparing for a meeting with the staff. 'We can't let these people go now!'

'We can't afford *not* to, Baby,' he shot back. 'I'm sorry. I dislike this even more than you do, but . . . well, we have no choice. You've spent hours pouring over those books. You can't argue that the reds beat the blacks in *this* color war!'

She slumped into a chair, crestfallen.

'Listen, honey, we're doing the best we can. At least we can stay open for the rest of the season. If the people who stay hussle their butts off, they can make more tips and we can still save our reputation.'

He frowned, his eyes level under drawn brows.

'Baby, I know what it feels like to be kicked out. It hurts. Hurts like hell. And it hurts me to be the one to do it.

'When I left the insurance business, it wasn't because I wanted a "career change" the way I told everybody. It was 'cause I was ousted, fired, given the old pink slip.

'How I hated having to come home and tell your mother. We covered it up for you and Lisa because, well, I guess because I was embarrassed. It probably would have been easier for you to grow up thinking your father wasn't perfect.'

At this, Baby burst into hysterical laughter, coughing and trying to stop herself.

'Dad, I'm sorry. I'm not . . . laughing . . . at you . . . it's just . . . it's just been such a hard day I guess I needed a good old belly laugh. I'm afraid I've grown up enough from your "baby" to know that no one, not even you, are or ever were perfect.'

Max's face drained.

'You mean you knew? And you didn't . . .'

'Dad, even a kid knows that things happen, things over which we have no control. If the roof hadn't leaked and the pool had been in better shape, if the fourth of July was hot and sunny instead of looking like we could use Noah and his Ark, we might be telling the kids tonight that they were all getting a raise.'

'I wish we *could* do that,' Max said, 'I hope you, at least, understand it.'

'I do, Dad. But I must tell you that your bookkeeping is a mess, that you spend entirely too much money on things that could be cut back and that, in a word, you've got to budget if you want to save Kellerman's, even after tonight.'

Max nodded, a tear in the corner of his eye.

'I call you "Baby", Miss Frances Kellerman. The truth is your old man is the real "baby" around here. Trying to be the life of the party and make my life a full time party. I guess it catches up with you after a while.'

'That's a hard thing to admit about yourself, Dad,' Baby said, as she ran and hugged him tightly around his neck. 'Especially to your daughter. But if you have the courage to do that – and I know it took courage – then you have the courage to pick up the pieces and make this place work. I know you can do it.

'When I was a kid, you'd always say, "Baby, I have faith in you. If anyone can do it, you can!" And I believed it. And I drew strength from it. Well the apple doesn't fall far from the tree, as they say, Dad. I know you can do it. And I'll help in any way I can!'

He hugged her again.

'You already have, honey. Having you here is probably the best thing that ever happened to me. I'm learning how to look at people through better eyes, thanks to you.'

'OK, so you're going to pick up the pieces,'
Baby said. 'But for now we have to go drop some,
as painful as it is. I don't know if I can face . . .

'We'll go together,' she said, as Max picked
up a stack of Kellerman LP records and Memory
Books from his desk and they walked out of the
office to the ballroom rehearsal hall.

Seven

A somber stillness replaced the usual gaiety of the ballroom rehearsal hall that night.

Although colorfully dressed in tight slacks and halter tops, or sexy t-shirts and jeans, the staffers had not gathered for fun. Some sat on the stage, nervously fingering an unlit cigarette. Others walked around aimlessly, sighing deeply with fears of what was to come.

Norman walked over to Neil, the lifeguard, who sat with his usual complacency on a chair by one of the tables. Neil never fitted in with the staffers, who enviously called him 'Joe College' and looked at his preppy slacks, shirts and sweaters with disdain.

Tonight was no exception. Neil was unconcerned about this meeting. He knew that his position was secure. No matter who else Max had to unload, *he* was not replaceable, lord of the pools, savior of the unskilled in the water.

Neil gave Norman a quick glance and tried to turn away.

'I wouldn't be asking, Neil but . . .' Norman started.

'No,' Neil said, getting up from his seat and walking across the room.

'Until Max pays us . . .' Norman begged, following Neil like a tall, skinny lost puppy dog.

'No,' Neil repeated, heartlessly.

'Neil, I'm completely broke!'

'Life's tough,' Neil observed. 'No loan, Norman.'

Norman was beyond desperate. Neil turned his back on him but he continued to follow him around. 'Look, I know we've never been buddy-buddy before or anything . . . but, Neil, please! Be a buddy!'

Neil shook his head. 'Shouldn't have spent all your dough on that girl,' he chastised Norman.

Norman's head fell. His shoulders drooped. But a tiny spark of joy remained in his eyes as he thought about that cute blonde, Tina. He looked up at Neil. 'No one ever looked at me that way before, Neil,' Norman admitted.

'What way?' Neil laughed. 'That dog was near-sighted!'

Norman turned red. He thought he was going to cry. 'Please, don't make me cry!' he said to himself. 'Not here! Not in front of the kids. Not in front of Neil!'

Just then, Tammy plopped down on a chair next to Norman and Neil.

'Frick and Frack,' she laughed, 'what're you two doing here? You're both probably safe from the dungeon's dragon.'

Neil unhappily held up a mimeographed sheet of paper which he'd been holding.

'We were invited,' he snarled. '*All* the staff was invited.'

Tammy shook her head and raised her own sheet of paper. 'Yeah, so what do you think? Are we being set up for the kill or what?'

'Well,' Neil smiled, 'there are some of us Max can't do without. Others? We'll just have to wait and see who is really of value around here.'

Tammy looked at Norman and made a face.

'Where did this cretin come from?' she asked. 'I think I'm going to be sick.'

'Just ignore Neil,' Norman said. 'He lives atop his own mountain like all self-respecting little gods. But I don't know about this meeting,' he admitted. 'I've got a bad feeling about this. I never knew of Mr Kellerman throwing his employees a party. Ever!'

Tammy shook her head in agreement as a wave of silence brought a hush across the room. Max walked in with Sweets and Baby, carrying a stack of Kellerman Albums and Memory Books.

'Evening everyone . . .' Max said tentatively. 'Having a good time?'

No one spoke.

'I'm sure you all want to know why I called you here.'

He looked around at the kids who nodded their heads in agreement.

'Well,' he tried to smile, 'there's the old good news-bad news joke. Something like Norman's routine!'

The kids laughed and Norman blushed. 'I'm not making fun of your routines Norman,' Max said. 'You're getting better all the time.' Now Norman beamed.

'Anyhow,' Max continued, 'the good news is . . . I have all your pay checks for last week!'

Shouts, cheers and applause greeted the announcement.

Max looked down. 'The bad news is . . . and I really do feel bad about this. I hope you kids can understand . . . Well, the bad news is, I can't keep paying all of you. I'm over my head in expenses and I know everyone is talking about it, so you must know too. I can't turn off the water or empty the pool but I have to cut back on staff.'

The kids looked around, panic on their faces, each wondering who would stay and who would go.

Max took a slip of paper from his pocket as Baby and Sweets watched awkwardly from behind him.

'So anyway, I made up a list here. I tried to do it fairly. I worked out a kinda point system for seniority, performance and such . . .'

'Come on, Mr Kellerman,' Tammy called out. 'You're killing us with the kindness already. Who are you gonna fire?'

Max sighed. 'Gimme a minute, OK? I brought along some Kellermans Albums and Memory Books for those of you who are going to have to go . . . so you'll have something to remember our wonderful times together.'

He looked down as he handed the Albums and Books to Baby and Sweets, put on his glasses, and held up the list.

'I want to thank everyone for . . . a great summer. OK, here's the list,' he said, as he began reading names.

In just a few minutes, it was over. Half the staff, including Penny, held Albums or Memory Books, the other half wore looks of discomfort or embarrassment because they did not. Neil remained smug, seated in the corner, no Album, no Book, in hand.

'Look . . .' Max stammered. 'I just want to say this wasn't easy . . . and . . . ah . . . good luck to all of you wherever you go!' He turned and walked briskly from the ballroom, followed by Sweets.

Baby hesitated and stood, hearing the grumbling from the group.

'Look,' she said to no one in particular, 'if you guys knew how bad both of us feel . . .'

'Give it a rest, OK?' Eddie said, as he held an Album.

'If there was anything I could do, you know I'd
. . .' Baby tried.

'Hey, Miss Management,' Rocco called out,
'why don't you just leave us alone, OK? You
don't belong here anymore.'

Baby looked at his angry eyes and scanned the
rest of the group. She felt a huge lump in her throat,
her head throbbed, and she gave up and walked
out. But she couldn't help noticing Johnny in the
corner with a tearful Penny, as he put his arms
around her and held her close to him.

Baby walked out the door, feeling very much
like an outsider looking in at the people who made
Kellerman's work.

'Where do I belong?' she asked herself.

Penny bit her lip and sobbed, throwing her
Album to the floor.

'Hey,' Johnny said, picking up the record, 'it's
cool, Penny. You're gonna stay. You'll take half
my salary, that's all.'

Norman stood nearby with Neil who watched
the scene with curious disdain.

'God,' Norman said, overhearing Johnny's offer
to Penny, 'is that romantic or what?'

'It's stupid, that's what it is!' Neil smirked, as
he turned and walked from the ballroom.

As he left, the strains of a soft, sad song
came from the record player. Someone had
put on music to soothe the fears and tears.
A slow dance. Gradually, the staff members
came together, starting to dance as a way of

saying goodbye or just getting rid of their grief.

Johnny took Penny into his arms and started to move her to the music. She looked at him and cried.

I can't take your money,' she shouted, breaking away.

'Why not? What're you talking about?' Johnny called, as she hurried from the room without answering him. He stood there stunned, then raced after her, out the ballroom door.

Penny ran down the path, across the grass sobbing. She stopped suddenly, when she heard the sound of footsteps behind her. As quick as a rattlesnake, she bolted across the bridge and up the steps to the staff area, running breathlessly to her cabin.

She ran in and slammed the door shut, locking the latch and leaning hard against it, clutching her Kellerman's album to her chest.

A moment later there was a knock at the door.

'Who is it?' she called.

'It's *me*!' Johnny shouted. 'What's going on with you? Let me in!'

She unlatched the lock and reluctantly opened the door.

'Penny? Why did you run from me?'

'I don't take charity.'

'Charity? From me! Penny, this is Johnny! You're my partner. You're my friend. You know how much I love you!'

She looked at him, her eyes spilling tears as she grabbed a suitcase from the top of her closet and opened it on the bed.

'Why won't you take it? Why? I know you'd do the same thing for me!'

She looked at him hard. 'It's true,' she thought. 'I would do it for him. But this is . . . this is different.'

'I need a real job – that's why,' she said to him, angrily.

'This isn't real?' Johnny asked.

'Johnny, I send half of what I make back to my family.'

'So do I,' he said. 'So what?'

'So how can I take half of what you get?' she cried.

'OK, OK, don't cry, duchess. You know I can't take it when you cry. All right, you won't take the money, then I'm not staying either!'

'Oh yes, you are,' she shouted, her dark eyes fiery and determined.

Johnny put his hands on her shoulders and sat next to her on the bed. 'You think I'm gonna go on here without you?' he asked gently. 'I can't and I won't.'

Penny smiled in spite of herself.

'OK . . . let's say you come with me . . . then what?' she asked.

'Then,' Johnny said, hesitatingly, 'we'll see.'

Penny's smile vanished.

'That's what you've always said. I want to know what's gonna . . . happen! What we're gonna . . . do. Move in together? Get married?'

Johnny stood up and started pacing around the tiny cabin.

He laughed, nervously. 'Is that what you want?' he asked.

'Yeah,' Penny said, 'yeah, one day . . . with somebody. It *is* what I want.'

He looked at her at a loss, refusing to make a commitment.

'Wait, I have a great idea,' he said. 'Really! Remember my old friend Flash Donetti from Jersey? He was that tall gorgeous blond guy. Italian as sauce but blond as a Swede. Anyhow, we always had this dream, this plan, that one day we'd hit the road. Just take off in a car and travel the country, work jobs here and there as we needed them and see the sights. It would be a great adventure. You and I might even be able to get nightclub gigs or something. And you'll love Flash when you really get to know him. He's terrific. The guy's a riot! What do you say?'

Penny shook her head.

'That's no adventure for me. That's being a gypsy, a nomad with no money and no future. No, Johnny, you and Flash might hit the road if you ever get the courage to leave your father some day, but figure me out of those plans. That's not a future, Johnny. That's an escape. An escape to nowhere. For both of us.'

Penny walked over and looked into his questioning eyes.

'Johnny, I don't have the same dreams as you do anymore, OK? When I dance with you, I do. When we dance I think of Vegas and shows and the big time. But when we're not dancing, when I really think about it . . .'

'Yeah?' Johnny pressed as a war of emotions raged through him.

'I want something . . . something else. I want a house, with kids and a husband who comes home at night! That's why it wasn't good when we were an item. You wanted it to be easy, loose, whenever. I wanted it to be . . . everything . . . to be forever. There's a big difference there, Johnny. And as much as we love each other in so many ways . . .'

'I thought it was pretty good,' Johnny interrupted, his face tight with strain.

'You know what I'm saying, Johnny. You and me . . . we're now, not forever. And it's probably too soon for both of us to even think about forever. Look, I gotta go. Maybe this thing is for the best. Maybe we'd just stay together because of the job and end up . . .

'Unless we're dancing together, the rest of it, it's too hard for me to be with you . . . it doesn't work,' she whispered, tormented by confusing emotions.

Johnny stood silently for what felt like years, overwhelmed by helplessness.

Unable to answer Penny the way she wanted him to frustrated and infuriated Johnny. But he knew in his heart he couldn't and he wouldn't.

'Fine! Great! Terrific!' he shouted as he looked at Penny regretfully, turned and stormed out the door, slamming it behind him.

As Johnny left Penny's cabin, Baby returned to her father's darkened office, depressed and still confused by the overwhelming mess of bookkeeping she had been unable to unravel.

She put on the old desk lamp, which cast weirdly-shaped shadows around the room. Baby shivered for an instant. 'I should have brought a sweater,' she thought. 'Too late now.'

She slumped down into the big old chair behind Max's desk and studied a pile of bills in front of her. She reviewed them one by one, over and over again, looking for a clue or a thread that would tie it all together.

'I feel like Sherlock Holmes,' she laughed. 'If I'm as lucky, I'll find the clues and solve the puzzle.'

Sighing deeply, she opened up the accounting ledger and began once again to go through the figures.

'There has to be something here,' she said to herself. 'Even Dad couldn't run Kellerman's into the ground so fast! There must be a mathematical error and I'm going to find it!'

Eight

When the dancing was over, the staffers straggled out of the ballroom, Albums in their hands, pausing for goodbye hugs as they headed to their cabins to pack.

Norman stood at the top of the porch stairs, sadly watching the gestures of friendship.

'I wish there was something we could do,' he said to Neil, who for some reason stayed and watched the partings, relieved, in spite of his confidence, that his job was secure.

'The die's been cast, Norman,' he laughed. 'That's life. There are winners and there are losers.'

'Tammy was right, Neil,' Norman said, 'you are a cretin! Don't you *care* about all this?'

Neil shrugged. 'Not really!'

Norman shook his head in disgust and turned away just as Ronnie, a pretty blonde dancer and waitress, walked up to him, holding an Album in her hand.

'So . . . I guess this is *sayanara*, Norman,' she smiled.

'Yeah,' Norman said self-consciously. 'So long, Ronnie. Good luck. I know you'll get a job. You're a great dancer!'

'I'll miss you, Norman,' she said softly.

Norman laughed. 'What are you talking about? Me? You'll miss me?'

'Sure,' Ronnie smiled demurely.

She leaned in and gave him a long, sweet kiss on the lips. When she drew back, Norman slowly opened his eyes and started to breathe again. He looked at her as though he was seeing a living angel.

'What'd you do that for, Ronnie?' Norman asked dreamily.

'I always wanted to,' she confessed. 'I was hoping you'd think of it first but . . .' She giggled. 'And now it looks like time's run out!'

Norman shook his head in disbelief. 'You always wanted to! Ronnie! I'm speechless. And for me, that's not easy! I didn't think you even knew my last name!' Norman blabbered as Neil watched in disgust.

'Sure I do. I even know your dog's name. Phyllis, right? I know everything you ever told me. Like, your favorite ice cream is chocolate, and you love mystery movies, and you don't ever put butter on your popcorn, and you'd give anything to be on a real New York stage!'

Norman shook his head. 'That's right! Then how come we haven't ever really . . . you know . . . talked until now?'

Ronnie blushed. 'I was afraid, Norman. You're so smart and talented. I didn't think I could keep up with you. You always think of something funny to say. Everyone knows you're a comic genius just waiting to be discovered. I'm just a little dancing girl waiting on tables. I figured you wouldn't be interested in me.'

'Not interested? . . . But you're so . . . beautiful! A goddess. A Venus de Milo disguised as a waitress who also is a terrific dancer. Ronnie, I think you're terrific!'

'Oh, gimme a break!' Neil called from the sideline.

'Get lost, Mumford,' Norman said. 'I don't see anyone pining over you, Dr Poolman.'

Norman turned to Ronnie. 'Look, you can't go. Not now. Not when we've just really found each other. You have to stay. We have to get to know each other better. Do you like chocolate ice cream?'

She smiled. 'My favorite!'

'That settles it,' Norman laughed. 'You can't go.'

'But I have to. I've been fired.'

'Wait . . . just wait one minute,' Norman said, as though a lightbulb went on in his head. 'What if I gave you half my salary . . . like Johnny's doing for Penny?'

Ronnie gasped. 'Norman, you'd do that for me?'

'Sure he would,' Neil laughed. 'He's a first-degree jerk!'

'No, he's not,' Ronnie smiled, kissing Norman warmly. 'He's a prince. The big jerk around here, Neil, is *you*!'

Ronnie looked into Norman's eyes again and leaned even closer, kissing him seductively. There was a tingling in the pit of her stomach. Norman nearly swooned.

Neil raised his eyes to the heavens in disgust, or perhaps, jealousy, and walked off.

After leaving Penny, Johnny went to the empty staff dance room. It was silent as he paced about, the clicking heels of his boots the only sounds other than those of the chirping crickets breaking the evening stillness.

He marched back and forth, aimlessly, trying to work out his confusion, his emptiness and sense of loss.

This room held so many memories, good memories of dancing, practicing new and daring dirty dances with Penny that at first even the kids had to get used to.

It was here where his emotions were unleashed and he finally felt free. He danced here with Baby, the other woman in his life, whose face he kept seeing as he thought about his discussion with Penny about the future.

Baby could never really be in his future, Johnny told himself. But she really wasn't Miss Management, either. That wasn't fair of Rocco to say.

She'd been there for the kids a lot of times. They'd never have had their show or been in the Bobby Darin warm-up routine without her influence on her father. She didn't deserve Rocco's dig.

And Johnny hadn't gone to her defense, he admitted to himself, feeling guilty. There was so much going on then. He couldn't believe it when Max read Penny's name from the list.

They were a team! They danced together. None of the other girls could take her place. But there it was, right on the list. Penny Lopez. And now she was packing to leave because Johnny knew, just knew, that he could not promise her more than dancing away the summer. He could not promise her the house and the kids she really wanted.

Why was it always so difficult? He fought with his father about working in the garage which he hated. It wasn't until his father had seen him dance for the very first time at the hotel last month that he finally understood Johnny's dream.

Dreams! His father had dreams too. He still marveled to think that his old man had been sought out by a Dodgers' scout! If only he'd known! So many bad feelings could have been avoided.

But there was no going back. He promised his father and himself that he would follow his dreams and he would. If Penny didn't really want that same dream, then . . .

Suddenly Penny walked into the room. He looked up at her, then looked away, too angry, confused, frustrated to hold her gaze.

Her eyes were soft and sad, apologetic. She did not speak. Instead, she walked to the record player and put on the song, 'These Arms of Mine', a soft, sultry tune to which they had created a special intimate dance. Johnny looked up at the sound of the music, surprised.

Penny walked over to him without saying a word. She stood in front as he watched her, suddenly swaying to the music, caught up in the emotion of the words and the rhythm. Johnny followed her, danced with her, performing the movements they had rehearsed so many times before. But this time was like no other time. They were saying goodbye. This was their last dance, but it was more than a dance. They were parting and, through the rhythm and the music, the movement, touching, bending and swaying, they were making love, the only way they ever would.

Nine

Norman was a man with a mission.

'If I can do it, you can do it,' he urged his fellow staff members as he stood in front of a crowd in the rehearsal hall. His eyes were bright, his face determined. Ronnie stood next to him, proud and encouraging, the perfect cheerleader.

'We're talking money, here, man,' Eddie complained. 'Hard cash. I can't afford to work for no charity.'

Several other staff members yelled a chorus of agreement. Norman raised his hands to silence them.

'Look,' he said, 'I know this is a sacrifice, but if we're really on our toes for the guests, then pool all the tips, we can make up a lot of the difference!'

Neil stood in the middle of the crowd, shaking his head negatively.

'What is this, a telethon or something? Look, it's life. Like I told you Norman, you have winners, you have losers. End of story.'

'It's the end of the story for you 'cause you're a "winner", right Neil?' Norman taunted. 'How would you feel if the shoe was on the other foot?

'Look, Max said he did his best to pick and choose who'd go and who'd stay, but there is no really fair way to do it. He knows that and so do we,' Norman said. 'So the bottom line is that half of us got a bum rap and the other half lucked out. I think we owe it to our friends to see that everyone gets a chance to finish out the summer with something!'

'I'm sorry, man, but I think for once in his life Joe College is the one who's actually making some sense,' Rocco argued. A buzz of voices hummed in apparent agreement.

'Wait a minute, Rocco. Didn't you just listen to what Norman said? About friends and helping your friends out. I thought you and Frankie were friends,' Ronnie said, pointing to Frankie who still clutched his Kellerman's Memory Book.

'You know it, we are,' Rocco said.

'Diane and Tammy . . . they're as tight as they come.'

'That's got nothin' to do with this!' Tammy shouted.

'Yes it does!' Ronnie yelled back over the discussions. 'If your friend is in trouble, you stand up for her, well, don't you? Don't you?'

The room went silent.

'Not unless you're a total patsy,' Neil said, breaking the silence.

'Yes, you do!' Norman said. 'You help them out. That's what we're talking about here, isn't it?'

'What you're talking about, man, is a fifty per cent pay cut. And I don't know no one who can afford that!' Rocco called out.

'Rocco, I couldn't agree more. No one really *can* afford it. But if it means we get to stay together,' Norman turned and looked toward Ronnie, 'I think it's worth it.'

Ronnie smiled proudly at Norman.

Neil moaned out loud. 'For God-sakes, I think you're brain dead,' he said, shaking his head and laughing.

Six-foot-three Eddie walked over toward Neil. 'Wait a minute, there, preppy. Maybe he's got something here.'

'You're not actually *buying* this crap, are you?' Neil asked incredulously.

'I don't know. I don't like it, but I do like being on the other side from you . . . I like that part a lot.'

Murmurs of agreement could be heard echoing across the room.

While the staff kids continued to discuss the pros and cons of following Johnny's lead in sharing his pay with Penny, the pair in question were still heavily into their final dance, feeling the strong sexual attractions that had kept them together for so long, but had remained an undercurrent until this unplanned parting.

The intensity of the dance made their vow to

be just dancing partners harder to resist. At the end of the dance, Johnny stared boldly, slowly and seductively at Penny. His gaze was riveted to her face, then moved over her whole body.

Penny felt herself tingle. Her heart throbbed. She ached to be crushed in his embrace. The smoldering flame she saw in his eyes pleased and ignited her.

Very gently and tenderly, Johnny took her face in his hands and kissed her. The sexual magnetism was overwhelming. Their bodies melded as Johnny gently eased Penny down on to the floor.

Suddenly the door flew open and Norman rushed into the room with Ronnie, Eddie, Rocco and other staff members behind him. They stood frozen in the doorway as they saw Johnny and Penny's intimate position.

'Oh my gosh, oh my golly!' Norman said.

'Oh, my golly?' Tammy repeated, laughing hysterically at Norman's reaction.

Penny straightened her halter top and sat up, staring at the group.

'So, uh, what do you guys want?' she asked, matter-of-factly.

Norman was in an embarrassed dither. 'I should've knocked,' he apologized. 'My mother always told me to knock. Not that I would have seen anything if I had . . .' he blabbered.

'What do you want, Norman?' Johnny asked, angrily, frustrated that his and Penny's moment had been spoiled.

'He figured it out,' Ronnie said excitedly, pointing to Norman. 'We're gonna do what you did for Penny . . . If everyone who's staying takes a cut . . . then we'll all be able to stay! Isn't it terrific!?'

'We convinced most of 'em,' Eddie said. 'We need you to do the rest.'

Johnny shook his head.

'OK, that's great. Now, could you guys leave us alone a minute, OK?'

'Sure . . . sorry,' Eddie said, as they backed out, closing the door behind them.

'Seems we're just to be dancing partners after all,' he smiled softly. 'Someone always gets in the way!'

She leaned back on the floor, half-smiling with regret.

'Looks like it,' she agreed.

Johnny leaned over Penny's face and stared deeply into her eyes. 'I just want you to know, no matter what you do, I love you,' he said, kissing her sweetly on the forehead.

Penny smiled and sat up.

'So . . . let's go convince whoever still needs convincing!'

'What're you saying, Penny?'

'You think I'm gonna starve by myself?' she smiled. 'At least here they feed us!'

He looked at her, hugged her tightly and took her hand. They slowly walked from the staff house together.

Ten

The single hold-out for the paysharing arrangement was Neil Mumford.

'We got to get 'em boys,' Johnny laughed. 'He's been waiting for this the *whole* summer.'

Eddie, Rocco and Norman chuckled as they followed Johnny's lead and marched toward the pool the following day.

'There he is,' Norman growled, 'Mr High and Mighty, sittin' up there in that lifeguard chair. Must be something about the air up there that makes the fellow dense.'

'It's not the air,' Rocco said. 'He's just an airhead. And a spoiled brat to boot. Time someone put the jerk in his place. And this might be the perfect time.'

Johnny smiled to the guests as they walked over toward the pool area, waving to dancing students and feeling for a minute like Max making his so-called rounds at every meal.

Johnny, Eddie and Rocco walked up to the

lifeguard chair where Neil was spreading some suntan oil on his arm.

'So,' Johnny called up to him. 'Looks like you're the only one still holding out on the fair-share arrangement, Neil. Pretty poor sportsmanship, old man, don't you say?' he mocked.

Neil ignored the trio and continued to spread the oil.

'So, you gonna give up half your pay so Eddie here can stay, or what?' Johnny asked.

Neil looked down and shrugged.

'Eddie? You think I care if Eddie stays or not?' He turned to all 260 pounds of Eddie and added, 'No hard feelings, of course.

Eddie shook his head. 'Absolutely not!'

Suddenly, a cry for help came from the pool. *'Help! Help!'* It was Norman, going under for the third time in the deep end.

'I can't . . . swim!' Norman shrieked, flailing about in twelve feet of water.

'I'm drowning! A cramp! *Help!'*

Neil stood up to dive in. Just as he was mid-air, Eddie and Johnny grabbed his swim trunks and pulled them off as he somersaulted into the water.

Norman swam to the edge of the pool and climbed out, laughing hysterically. Neil surfaced and swam to the edge, remaining in the water, his face livid.

'You cretins! Gimme back my trunks!'

'Now who's the cretin?' Norman laughed.

'You gonna join the group and take a cut?' Johnny asked, dangling the trunks in mid-air.

'No way!' Neil shouted. The group turned, trunks in hand, and started to walk away.

Neil pounded the water as a crowd began to gather to see what all the excitement was about.

'Wait a minute!' Neil yelled. 'Wait! All right! All right! I'll do it!'

The guys stopped in their tracks and turned toward the pool.

'You're sure?' Johnny asked. 'I mean, if you're lyin', there's other things we could do . . .'

'I'm sure,' Neil snapped, gritting his teeth. 'Just gimme my suit and get the hell out of here!'

They threw the trunks back to Neil cheered, and ran laughing from the pool.

In spite of the staffers' own resolution of the problem, Baby had refused to give up her personal quest for a solution.

Still dressed in clothes from the previous night, she sat crosschecking a pile of cancelled checks with the ledger. Suddenly she picked up a check and her heart skipped a beat. She quickly flung back several pages in the ledger and made a note on the legal pad at her side.

She jumped from the unexpected noise as Robin suddenly barged into the office.

'That's it! I quit!' Robin shouted, throwing down her apron. 'I cannot put up with the small-minded, petty, condescending attitude of this clientele,' she shouted, ranting and raging around the room.

'Baby, I don't know how you did it this long. Why these people! I am *never* repeat *never*, working here again and I will *never* be the Kellerman in the family to see that his hotel name never dies. This work is horrible.'

Baby kept working on the ledger as Robin rampaged around the room, her arms flailing, her frizzy hair flying wildly.

'This woman wants to know what the special of the day is. So I tell her, because you said "the customer is always right" and to think *I believed you*! Anyway, I tell her we have "very special" tuna fish. Then she gets very weird and says she doesn't want tuna, she's allergic or some stupid thing, she wants a Waldorf salad. Have you ever heard of it? I never did.'

Baby continued to flip back and forth between checks and pages in the ledger as Robin rambled on.

'So, she tells me in this incredibly obnoxious voice which I'll try to imitate, but I could never be *that* obnoxious, that it's a very famous salad made with mayonnaise, apples, celery and walnuts.'

Baby looked up for a minute at Robin's imitation and smiled.

'Well, I told her "that sounds really disgusting!" And then she gets mad at me! Tells me I have no class. Can you imagine *that*! Tells me to get her a Waldorf salad or she'll have me fired! Can you believe it! *She'll have me fired*! A Kellerman! Well! That's it! I quit! No more! No way!'

'Fine,' Baby answered. 'It's time for you to move up anyway, Robin. Grab a pad. We've got work to do here.'

'Did you even hear one word I said?' Robin asked. 'I am hysterical over this miserable, intolerable woman, *obnoxious* woman and her Waldorf salad, which does sound disgusting, doesn't it? And you tell me to get a pad and pencil. Honestly, I don't know what's gotten into you, Baby.'

'Congratulations, Robin, you've just been promoted. Tomorrow I'll be back at that station. Now write this down!'

Hours later, Baby dragged Robin out of Max's office and back to the cabin.

'I don't know where you get your energy, Baby. I'm going to sleep!' Robin said.

'Sleep? How can you sleep after we just made the discovery that will save this hotel? Take a shower and let's go celebrate,' Baby said.

'No, thanks. I'm really dead. I'll celebrate tomorrow. Shower's yours.'

Before Baby had put on her bathrobe, Robin was fast asleep, uniform and all, snoring her nose off.

Baby showered and changed quickly, switched off the lights and raced over to the main building. She found Max standing at the bar, drowning his sorrows as Sweets played a sorrowful tune on the piano.

'Sweets! Change that tune! Strike up the band,' Baby called, as she bounced into the bar. 'Everything's going to be all right!'

'What are you talking about?' Max asked, after downing a shot glass filled to the rim with whiskey.

'Baby, what's up?' Sweets asked. 'Tell us fast before your Daddy's gonna pass out!'

'You books were a mess. I told you that when I first looked at them. And it seemed you were spending an awful lot for certain things. Well when I went back and reviewed it piece by piece, I found you'd paid for the roof twice! And your last bookkeeper added a few zeroes where they shouldn't have been!'

Max grabbed her hand, his face pale. 'Are you sure, Baby?'

'Positive,' she beamed. 'Actually, you're ahead!'

'Ahead!' Max nearly keeled over. I'm *ahead*! I've *never* been . . . in my whole life . . . How much?' he asked breathlessly.

'Eight dollars and twenty-three cents,' Baby laughed.

'Oh.' Max's face fell.

'Well,' he smiled, rallying at the good news, 'I'm eight bucks closer to being a millionaire, right?'

'Right!' Baby laughed, as she hugged her father.

'Come on,' Max said jubilantly. 'Let's go tell the kids.'

'Congratulations, Baby,' Sweets beamed. 'I knew if anyone could do it, it would be you.

You are a very special woman. I'm proud of you!'

Baby hugged Sweets. 'Thanks, I needed that,' she smiled.

Max and Baby walked across the moist evening grass toward the staff quarters.

'I'm so relieved about this,' he sighed. 'I can't thank you enough for being a genius,' he said to his daughter.

She smiled. 'No thanks necessary, Dad. That's what family is all about.'

'Well, thanks, anyhow,' he smiled, reaching out to hug her.

The strains of 'Work It Out' blared from the staff quarters as they walked across the bridge and up the stairs to the cabins on the far side.

Inside the dance room spirits were high, everyone united in their energy and relief, releasing the anxiety of the past few days and celebrating the comraderie that was keeping them together.

Johnny danced with Penny, laughing and fooling around until another guy cut in as Johnny gave Penny a spin around. Johnny grinned, surrendering her as he moved back and leaned against the wooden wall watching the exciting frenzy.

'It's so great what we have here,' he thought to himself. 'All these people, so different, but finally, in the end, willing to do what even family members won't sometimes.'

Johnny felt a lump in his throat, a real affection for the kids he lived and worked with, danced and played with, and now, finally, shared his livelihood with. He walked out onto the porch and took a deep breath of fresh air.

The loud pulsating music blared from the dance room forcing Johnny to clap his hands, snap his fingers and finally sing along, loud and energetically, even if a little off-key.

Suddenly he saw Baby and Max emerge from the dark pathway.

'Ah, it's management again. What's the matter, Mr Kellerman, afraid we're goin' to break into the Coke machine?'

'C'mon Johnny,' Max said 'I know you're mad at me. I understand. But I have good news.'

'Whatever it is, I've got better. The staff, well, we all got together, thanks to Norman, and decided to share our pay. So nobody's got to lose his job!'

'You all agreed to that?' Max asked in amazement.

'Look, that's really wonderful,' Baby said, 'but . . .'

Max interrupted her. 'Now, wait a minute, here, Baby. Let's think this through. If they really want . . .'

Baby froze him silent with an icy glance.

'The books were wrong, Johnny,' Baby said, taking over for her father. 'Everybody can stay on full salary.'

'How did this happen?' Johnny asked, his eyes lighting up with delight.

'Baby . . .' Max started.

'My dad figured it out,' Baby interrupted. Max and Baby looked at each other and smiled.

Johnny looked at both of them.

'Well I'm glad someone did,' he said. 'Mr Kellerman, I owe you an apology.'

Max smiled. 'Thanks Johnny. Consider us even.'

'You know everybody is feeling really great in there to begin with tonight,' Johnny said. 'After your announcement, this is gonna turn into a hell of a party!'

'I hope so,' Max smiled. 'You guys deserve it.' He headed into the dance room, followed by Johnny. Baby stood outside, reluctant to go in. Johnny turned around and saw her waiting. He came back out, a puzzled expression on his face.

'Hey, come on! This is your party, too, you know,' he smiled.

'Thanks,' she said. 'But I don't really belong in there. You know, Miss Management and all. But thanks anyway. I think it's really great, incredibly wonderful really, that even if we hadn't found the money the kids would have stayed on at the hotel. It would have killed me and Dad to lose the place after it's been in the family so many years.

'But the solidarity, the caring that would make everybody share . . . that's really special, Johnny.

I'm glad to hear about it and gladder still that you won't have to do it!'

'Look, that Miss Management crack wasn't very fair. You couldn't help it. You probably are the one who fixed it up. I'm sorry I didn't tell Rocco off when he said it. I know it's not true,' Johnny said sincerely.

'It was the truth, OK? Can't help it if I'm a Kellerman. I'm just glad everything will work out and the kids can stay.'

'But . . .' Johnny stammered, as he stopped himself from saying, 'I know you're a Kellerman and that probably puts you out of my reach!'

'So, see you tomorrow,' Baby smiled, wanly, and rushed away toward the darkened path. Johnny heard the sounds of the staff cheering to Max's announcement and the music and cheering grew even louder as he stood outside watching Baby's figure disappear into the dark shadows.

'She should be here,' he said to himself. 'Should I go after her?'

But his legs didn't take him. 'How can Johnny from Jersey make the boss's daughter understand?' he thought.

As he went to join the celebration he closed his eyes for a moment and remembered his sweetest encounter with Baby, dancing together feeling a oneness they hadn't had time for again. How could they ever make it happen again?

Eleven

With the financial pressures off, the kids faced the last half of the summer at Kellerman's with energy and determination.

Johnny and Penny were in the ballroom rehearsal hall early the next morning, working on a routine in progress to the pop hit, 'Kansas City'. Both were focused and intense on their movements, their bodies dripping with sweat.

As the music played, Johnny was off in another world, thoroughly involved, thinking on his feet, moving Penny around and changing movements as they went.

He stopped suddenly, frustrated, shaking his head. 'This beat is off!' he shouted to Penny, who wiped her brow with a handkerchief.

'It's almost too hot to think,' she said, as the music continued to play in the background. 'Maybe we should take five,' she suggested.

'We don't have time. We gotta get this right!' Johnny said harshly. 'It's gonna be ninety-nine degrees in here no matter *when* we try it. So we stay and get it right. Now.'

Penny bit her lower lip, trying to quiet her anger.

Suddenly, T.C., Jay and Cecily ran into the room, distracting Penny from Johnny's foul mood. T.C. held up a 45 and headed excitedly straight for the record player.

'Johnny, you gotta hear this man. It's so hot! It's gonna cook the country,' T.C. called out. 'One 'a my brothers recorded it.'

Johnny wiped his brow and looked curiously at T .C.

'The heat got you, man? You don't have no brother,' Johnny said, as T.C. took the 'Kansas City' record off the machine and replaced it with the new 45.

'Hey, come on, man what're you doing?' Johnny shouted. 'We're working here!' He headed for the record player, angrily ready to pull off the disc, then stopped in his tracks as he listened to the strains of James Brown's song 'Night Train' that T.C. had put on.

'So, what d'you think?' T.C. smiled.

Johnny smiled slowly. 'I think your brother's got somethin' here.' He motioned to the dancers. 'Come on, see if you can catch this.'

Johnny walked back to Penny, who had calmed down herself now and was caught up by the music. Together they started the routine again as T.C. and the others joined them, trying to follow.

The music was perfect. The movements slid into place. Johnny closed his eyes and gave into the beat, letting the rhythm inspire him to move, twist, bend and sway as Penny and the others tried to follow his lead.

The music continued when Johnny suddenly looked up, about to go into a turn. He stopped dead in his tracks. Penny followed his gaze and both sets of eyes fell upon Johnny's old friend Flash Donetti standing in the doorway with Baby, grinning.

Baby walked in, apologizing. 'I told him you were working, but . . .' she said to Johnny who stood staring at the handsome tough-looking blond guy in his early twenties who grinned from ear to ear. He was wearing torn jeans and a t-shirt, and a duffle bag was slung over his shoulder.

'How you doin' Ace?' Flash asked.

'Depends on what *you're* doin' here. What d'you want? Money? An alibi?'

Flash just grinned his toothy, irresistible smile.

'Just wanted to check you out . . . see if you were still spinnin' around on those little twinkle toes of yours.'

Johnny laughed and flashed his own irresistible smile back. 'You're not careful, I'm gonna check out some of your teeth!' he threatened, smiling broadly as he walked up to Flash.

'Come 'ere, you!'

The two friends reached out and hugged.

'I can't believe it's you!' Johnny said. 'Penny and I were just talking yesterday about you and

me and our screwball "hit the road" plan when
we were kids.'

Flash's face darkened momentarily, but Johnny
didn't notice. He grabbed him once more in a bear
hug, dragging him by the neck toward the kids.

'Everyone, this is my worst half – Flash Donetti.
Flash this is my dancing partner, Penny Lopez,
Jay, T.C., Cecily, and you already met Baby,
didn't you?'

Flash glanced at Baby and smiled. 'Baby?'

'It's a nickname my father gave me,' she said
as color rose up her neck to her cheeks.

'I like it. . . Baby,' Flash said, smiling seductively.
'My little Baby doll . . .'

Johnny pulled him by the arm. 'Cool it, buddy!'
he warned.

'Relax, Johnny. I'm cool,' Flash smiled.

'Well, shower or something, Flash. Get cooler.'

'What else is there to do around this place?'
Flash laughed. 'Sweat it out over a really strict
game of shuffle board?'

Johnny shook his head and roared with laughter, throwing his arm around Flash's neck.

'You never change, do you, buddy? You're as
crazy as you were in third grade!'

Twelve

'Let's see if your handball's improved since the old neighborhood,' Flash challenged Johnny. 'Or don't they play manly games up here in the fancy woods?'

'Hey, lay off it, man,' Johnny said. 'Sure we can play. Come on.'

They walked over to the asphalt backboard and started an intense game of one of the favorite street sports – handball. Both were equally good, rough, tough and tenacious.

'Glad to see you haven't lost your touch, Ace,' Flash called out as he slammed the ball against the wall, returning Johnny's serve.

'I can cream you anytime,' Johnny shouted back, slamming the ball with an extra show of force.

'I was beginning to wonder,' Flash smiled.

'What?' Johnny looked up at his old friend.

'Whether you'd turned sissy or anything, you know those twinkle toe boys,' he smirked.

Johnny dropped the ball and glared at Flash, frowning.

'Try me,' Johnny challenged.

Flash grinned and came at him. They wrestled on the hot pavement, each struggling to bring the other to the ground as they rolled and pushed, grunted and shoved. Finally Johnny tripped Flash and toppled him to the ground.

Flash sat on the steaming asphalt breathing heavily, winded from the conflict.

'You been working out or what?' he asked curiously.

'I been working,' Johnny said harshly. 'Period.'

Flash stood up and dusted off his pants. 'Me too,' he smiled.

Johnny looked at him dubiously.

'Yeah? You been working? Doing what?'

'I had a gig in Fuderman's hardware store. So I go and make fun of the guy's name and he gets pissed off. What a jerk. Then he nabbed me stealing some paint. So that was the end of old Flash's career at Fuderman's. To top it off, I got into a thing with my old man and he kicked me outta the house. Can you believe it? This has not been my lucky summer.'

'Sounds like some great summer, all right,' Johnny agreed.

'It was better in the old days, wasn't it Johnny? Boy, we had some good times,' he laughed. 'I ran into Freddy Benino the other day. Remember when we beat the crap outta him, hung him up to dry in the cleaners, sent him rollin' round that rack?'

Flash laughed hysterically, recalling the prank.

Johnny gave a small smile. 'The guy was an animal,' he admitted. 'He deserved worse.'

After a moment, he looked at Flash. 'That was a good time for you, huh?'

Flash caught Johnny's look. 'OK, it was stupid. But that's why we made our plan . . . get on that highway, let it take us wherever it was going . . . remember that?'

'We were sixteen, Flash,' Johnny said 'That's a lotta years ago.'

'So?' Flash looked confused by Johnny's remark. 'You ready or what?'

Johnny looked down for a moment.

'Hey, buddy, we're big boys now! I've made other plans since I was sixteen.'

'So break 'em,' Flash said simply, not understanding Johnny's meaning. 'I came to get you, man. That's why I came . . .'

'Things change, buddy,' Johnny said, looking at him with difficulty.

Flash was momentarily speechless in his surprise. 'You mean you're not comin' with me??' He looked at Johnny in shock.

Johnny held Flash's gaze. A suffocating sensation filled his chest as he saw Flash's reaction and he turned away, unable to answer.

Flash took a deep breath, a look of pained tolerance, even acceptance, on his face.

'OK, forget it. No big deal,' he said, a cold dignity creating a stony mask on his face.

Johnny stood up, grabbing Flash by the arm as he started to walk off the court.

'Look, why don't you hang out here a while?' Johnny offered. 'I got plenty of space in my cabin.

Flash looked around and laughed. 'I don't think so,' he said soberly.

'Come on. You can check out the chicks. We'll party!' Johnny tempted him.

Flash grinned his old smile. 'You hadda say it. The magic word for old Flash, huh? OK, why not? There's one chick, a little bitty Baby one, I wouldn't mind partying with at all!'

Johnny's eyes darkened at that but he let it pass, trying to save the friendship that his decision had almost ruined.

The two friends walked off the court back toward the staff quarters as Flash recounted his escapades as the funniest guy at Fuderman's.

Thirteen

The big attraction at Kellerman's that afternoon was Swami Lou, the renowned palm reader and fortune teller and the center of attention for a crowd of curious and skeptical guests on the patio.

The Swami sat on a dais in the center of the patio, surrounded by tables of guests seated for lunch, many of whom were more interested in his predictions for one young lady's future than the blinztes and sour cream on the menu that day.

'I see exciting things for you in your new marriage,' the Swami told the young woman, his eyes closed, as his fingers ran up and down her small hands touching a shiny wedding band and large diamond ring.

'He's really got them in the palm of his hands, hasn't he?' Max laughed to Baby, as they watched from the side of the dais.

Baby winced at the play on words.

'I can't help it,' Max smiled. 'I'm a born entertainer.'

The Swami continued to hold the young woman's hands as he pressed his eyes closed tighter and called for silence.

'You will be careful not to tell your husband how to run his business, he will stay out of the kitchen, and you will both be happy!' the Swami concluded as he opened his eyes to the applause of the audience and the beaming smile of the young woman whose hands he still held.

'Swami Lou, ladies and gentlemen. Isn't he terrific! Thank you, thank you. And a special thank you to our guest Laura who graciously volunteered to have her palm read. A round of applause for Laura!'

The guests gave a polite hand for Laura who blushed a beet red and slid into her seat.

'I want to do it, I want to do it,' Robin whispered to Baby, standing next to her at Baby's waitress stand. After the hotel's financial disaster was behind them, Robin swiftly returned her uniform to Mary in central supply and swore she would never do that kind of work again!

'I could use a hint about my future, though,' Robin whispered.

Max was at the microphone, congratulating Swami Lou for his performance and detailing his availability to guests for the day. 'Now, if any of you don't agree with your readings,' Max pointed out 'just ask the Swami to read your *other* palm, maybe he'll do better,' Max smiled. 'We all know there's *two sides* to every story!'

He roared with laughter as the Swami took yet another bow.

The guests chuckled and rolled their eyes.

'That Max,' one old lady smiled. 'He never gives up his shticks. Still thinks *he's* going to be discovered as a comic in the Catskills here like Henny Youngman!'

Her friend nodded in agreement as she stuffed her mouth with blintzes.

'And tomorrow as a special treat, Swami Lou will hypnotize a few adventurous volunteers and send them into another dimension entirely,' Max said, enticing a hub of discussion across the patio on the truth or fiction of other dimensions.

'Oh, Baby,' Robin cried, 'let's volunteer!'

'I can't. I'm staff,' Baby smiled. 'You do it. Since you turned in your uniform, you're a civilian again!'

Robin hesitated. 'I don't know if I'm ready for another dimension . . . unless I'll have blonde hair and a bigger wardrobe,' she babbled, day-dreaming of changing her lifestyle.

As Robin spoke, Flash suddenly appeared at their sides, ignoring Robin but smiling pointedly and suggestively at Baby.

'Hi,' he said, staring straight into Baby's eyes. 'There's a party tonight . . . staff quarters around eight. See you there, OK?'

Baby gasped, taken aback by his sudden appearance and invitation and somewhat uncomfortable with his tough, though attractive, manner.

'I really don't think I . . .' she stammered.

Flash put his hands on her shoulders and straightened the collar of her waitress uniform, as chills ran up and down Baby's spine. She felt her face flush at the same time.

'You ain't gonna turn me down, now, are you, missy?' he asked.

'No,' she said, hastily adding, '. . . I mean, I . . .'

'Great,' Flash smiled that seductive grin. 'See ya there.'

He walked off as Robin stared after him. She turned to Baby, whose face looked kind of dreamy.

'And you kept this from me?' Robin nearly shouted.

'I just met him, Robin, honest,' Baby laughed. 'He's Johnny's old friend from New Jersey. Wants to travel around the country or something. He's really not my type.'

'Are you crazy, Baby! He's adorable! Did you see that smile? And he looks dangerous . . . I *love* that look. This could be a major growth experience for you!'

Baby walked away laughing. 'Oh, Robin, please!'

Robin chased after her. 'I want to hear everything – absolutely everything, I mean it! I'll be waiting up for you . . .' Robin said with a twinkle in her eye.

Baby shook her head. 'That girl is too much! She's worse than a mother would be!' She stopped and smiled to herself.

'Actually, she's pretty terrific,' she thought. Baby turned to watch her slightly overweight, waiting-to-blossom cousin head into the dining room. 'There's not a jealous bone in that girl's body.'

That night, the staff dance room was packed, the gaiety of the past few days still in the air as couples walked around arm in arm or necked in not-too-dark corners.

The gang was hanging around between dances, catching up on the gossip of the day or talking to friends they hadn't seen during work hours.

'So I said to her,' Hank told his buddy Frank, ' "you wanna go out with me or you wanna call your mother first?" ' causing Frank to explode into gales of laughter.

Nearby, Joanne and Cecily were deep in conversation, talking about famous ladies and their figures. 'Well, look at Jackie Kennedy,' Joanne said, 'she had kids and she's still attractive . . .'

Leaning against the wall, Stephen and D.A. were more interested in talking about cars than women for a change.

'It was a '53 Vette, man . . . bored and stroked to 302 . . . a real rocket . . .'

Standing near Stephen and D.A., Flash and Johnny reminisced about the good old times, when the music started up again with Dionne singing 'The Wanderer'.

'You don't remember Teddy Franklin?' Flash
yelled to Johnny over the sound of the music.
'Well, anyway, we went down to Rigley's bar
. . . had a few beers and, man, it was all over!
We tore up the place so bad . . .' Flash roared.
Johnny smiled slightly.

Just then, Stephen pulled Johnny away from
Flash as the kids broke into a wild and feverish
dance.

'Come on,' Stephen cried. 'Let's do it!'

Before Flash knew what was happening, Johnny was in the midst of the other dancers, leading
them in a down-driving dirty dance routine to 'The
Wanderer', smiling and happy, lost in the spell of
the music.

Flash stood forgotten.

But he continued to watch the group of friends –
Johnny's new friends he thought grimly – isolated
and blue.

Johnny was oblivious to Flash's presence as
the heat of the dance intensified. Everyone in
the room but Flash was moving. The longer he
watched, the more uncomfortable Flash became.
Finally, near the end of the song, he walked out
of the room. No one noticed.

As the music to 'The Wanderer' ended, Johnny
and the other kids cheered with happy exhaustion. A slow tune followed and some of the kids fell
into each other's arms and slowly moved around
the stifling room, sweat pouring from them, but
satisfaction on their faces. Some headed out to

the porch for some fresh, although still hot, air.
Johnny looked around for Flash, pushing through
the crowds of dancing couples to see if he might
have found himself a chick for this, his kind of sexy
dancing. When he didn't see him inside, Johnny
headed out to the porch.

'Hey man,' Johnny called. 'Where'd you go?
That was a hot number, you should've jumped in!'

Flash stood alone in a corner of the porch.
Johnny registered his dark mood and walked over
slowly, smiling to himself.

He took Flash by the arm and pulled him out
of the corner and over to the other dancers on
the porch.

'Hey everybody, you don't know this, but me
and my friend Flash, there was this thing we
used to do in this guy Marty's basement . . .' he
started.

'A science project, I bet,' Norman laughed, as
he held his arm around Ronnie's waist.

'Very good Norman,' Johnny mocked. 'Hey,
Hank, Rocco . . . come here,' he called.

Flash pulled Johnny aside as the two guys
approached. 'Hey, I don't wanna do this man,'
he said uncomfortably, his face taught and
grim.

'Sure you do,' Johnny smiled, pulling him back
toward the rest of the guys.

Johnny, Flash, Rocco and Hank huddled on the
steps of the porch for a few minutes as the group
looked on perplexed.

Every so often they'd punch one another or guffaw about something. Finally, the four turned toward the group from the top step of the porch, finding their pitches, and started to sing a doo-wop version of 'Why Do Fools Fall In Love?'.

The kids loved it, clapping and singing along. As they sang, Flash got more and more into it, beginning to enjoy himself, as his face relaxed and his eyes twinkled.

Toward the big end of the song, Baby approached the dance bungalow and Flash spotted her, happy now, as he hammed it up with the other guys, exaggerating his voice and movements, getting down on his knees and singing the last few bars of the tune directly to Baby.

Fourteen

The performance ended with a flourish and the kids went wild, running up to the four singers like groupies after a rock concert.

Flash slipped off the side of the porch and walked directly over to Baby. 'I'm glad you came,' he smiled, looking into her eyes.

Baby felt her heart flutter in spite of herself.

'You were great!' she said, trying to change the subject.

'Did you guys practise that or was it improvisational?'

'Improvi-what?' Flash looked confused.

'I mean, did you just do it all of a sudden, without practising?' she explained gently.

'Oh, yeah, Johnny and me used to do it with these guys back in Jersey all the time. We had these dreams that we were going to be discovered, become big hits like Dionne and the Belmonts or something, ya know? But that's just dream stuff. It never happens. Nothin' comes from singing in some guy's basement.'

Baby shook her head. 'That's not necessarily true,' she disagreed. 'People have to start some place. Lots of groups who sang in their basements are famous today, maybe not as many as would like to be, though, I'll agree with that. But it's important to have a dream, to work for something. Like Johnny and his dancing. He's fantastic and he's working toward his goal by being here. I give him a lot of credit for that,' she said.

Flash's face darkened at the mention of Johnny's dancing and Baby realized she might have gone too far.

'Listen,' she said, taking him by the hand. 'I came here to a dance tonight, right?'

His expressive face changed and became almost happy. 'Yeah, you did. And because I asked you, too. So why don't we dance?' He led her into the bungalow where a slow dance was playing on the record player.

Johnny was dancing with Penny when he noticed Flash and Baby together. He could see that his friend was putting on the moves, holding Baby tight, moving his hands up and down her back and arms, whispering into her ear and making her laugh every so often.

A troubled look crossed Johnny's face as he led Penny over toward Flash and Baby.

Johnny looked at Flash. 'What'd you say we switch partners, partner? Penny's been dying to dance with you all night.'

Penny's eyebrows raised slightly as she smiled and moved quickly into Flash's arms as Johnny pulled Baby to his side.

Baby looked up at Johnny also with surprise. He moved her slowly and expertly around the floor.

'What was that all about?' she asked.

Johnny grimaced. 'Could you do me a favor?' he asked. 'Let him find someone else to be with tonight.'

'Why?' Baby asked. 'He invited me.'

'Look, he's my old buddy and all that, but I know the guy and . . . and I think he has the wrong idea about you and . . . he's never met a girl like you before . . .' Johnny stammered.

'And he's your friend and it bothers you,' Baby finished as Johnny's words trailed off.

'Yeah, kind of,' he said, holding her close so that she could smell his after shave. Her heart beat loudly, louder than she wanted it to.

Johnny held her close as he whispered in her ear. She found his nearness exciting and disturbing, but mostly confusing.

'Yeah, I mean . . . the kind of girls he's used to . . . You're just not . . . that kinda girl.'

Baby pulled back and looked into Johnny's eyes.

'Is that good?' she asked mischievously.

'Yeah,' Johnny smiled. 'I guess it is. It's real good. For you. And for me, too, because I got to know that there were girls like you. But Flash

. . . he won't understand and I don't want you to get hurt.'

'So . . . you want me to go?' she asked, looking toward Flash and Penny, entwined in a sexy move as the song was coming to an end.

'I don't know what to say . . , I . . .'

'It's OK,' Baby said, as Johnny squeezed her hand. 'Say goodbye to him for me, will you?'

'Sure,' Johnny smiled, feeling his own heart pound.

Baby smiled at Johnny, glanced at Flash, turned and walked quickly out of the room. Instantly, Flash was at Johnny's side.

'Hey, man, what happened to my date?'

'She . . . had to split,' Johnny lied.

'Why?'

Johnny turned, avoiding Flash's gaze and walked over to the sofa in the corner of the room. He flopped down. Flash did the same, sitting next to Johnny.

'Hey, man,' Flash said angrily, 'I'm askin' you what happened to my date. She was my woman tonight. She came to see me. Then you switch partners and vamoose, she's gone. What's up!'

'She doesn't belong here, Flash. She's different.'

'You mean she doesn't belong with me?' Flash asked, his eyes ablaze with fury.

'She's the boss's daughter for God's sake, Flash,' Johnny said. 'Leave it alone.'

'What's your problem with me, man?' Flash asked Johnny.

'No problem.'

'Yeah, there is. I saw it the minute I got here. You think you're something special, some kind of a leader or big shot, cause you teach a bunch 'a waiters and busboys how to dance?'

Johnny's eyes flashed with sudden rage.

'What do *you* know about that?'

'I know you're kiddin' yourself . . . You and me . . . we're *just people*, plain old common people. The best that's gonna happen to us is we hit the road, we get on Route 80 and fly, man . . .'

Flash pulled an old map out of his hip pocket. It was tattered and frayed, but one bold red line running across it stood out, covering the tracks of Route 80 from coast to coast.

'I still got the map, Johnny,' Flash said excitedly, pointing to the red line. 'There's our route, our road to the future . . . right there!'

Johnny looked at the map and sighed. A sadness crossed his face and he leaned back on the old, lumpy couch, pulling his neck up and staring at the ceiling, a look of sadness crossing his face.

Flash winced as he caught Johnny's reaction.

'But, like you said . . . things change,' Flash growled as he jumped up, stuffed the map in his pocket and ran out of the room before Johnny could stop him.

Johnny jumped up and ran after him, his face contorted with pain and confusion.

'Wait up, will ya, Flash?' he called as he walked out onto the porch.

Flash stopped at the bottom of the steps.

'Hey, look, I'm sorry, buddy,' Johnny said, his voice choked with emotion.

'Forget it. You're right. It ain't like the old days,' Flash said curtly. He looked at Johnny. 'You really think you owe these people, huh?'

Johnny shook his head and sat on the step. 'I don't know. Maybe I owe myself,' he admitted.

'Great. Fine. So you found somethin' good. You should stick with it,' Flash said, sitting down, too.

'You think it's a joke,' Johnny laughed dryly, 'you think I'm a joke. You don't get it, do you?'

Flash looked at Johnny straight on. 'You're wrong, man,' he said, 'you're wrong about me.

'You got a life. That's all that matters. I hope it works out for you. I really do. But I got to find one for myself, see? I always thought it was out there somewhere. Out on the road, or in a small town. Some place where I could feel important. Do something that other people needed. You found that here. You're lucky, man.

'I just never grew up,' Flash laughed. 'And I guess, when I wasn't watching you, Johnny, you went and grew up on me.'

Johnny smiled sadly. He reached into his pocket and pulled out his car keys, holding them out to Flash.

'Take them,' he said softly.

'What?' Flash looked confused.

'You'll be in Ohio by the morning. You never know where your special place will be until you go and find it. If I can't go with you, the least I can do is give you the chance to follow your dream. We made a pledge. Take it. Send me a postcard and tell me what it looks like.' Johnny laughed. 'You know, I've never been further west than Jersey?'

'So come with me,' Flash begged excitedly. 'It's not too late. Maybe you could put your dream to work out there. Dance in Vegas or something. God I've always wanted to go to Vegas!'

Johnny shook his head.

'We've got to get to our own dreams on our own, Flash. But you deserve the chance to go after yours. Just don't go making fun of some guy's name or bustin' up bars from coast to coast. That's not going to get you anything but trouble.

'Go on, take the car. But take it to find a good life. You deserve it, buddy. I'm sorry I'm letting you down and not going with you.'

Flash looked at Johnny.

'I came for you, man. Not to steal your car.'

The two old friends stood up as Johnny remained, hands outstretched, with the keys in his hands. He stared at Flash, a silent plea in his eyes.

Inside the dance bungalow, the music blared and the kids got their nightly release from the heat and exhaustion of work. The music played on long into the night.

When Baby returned early to the cabin Robin was surprised to see her.

'What are you doing here? It's only nine o'clock.' she asked. 'What happened? Did he make any moves? Tell me. What happened?'

'Nothing,' Baby said, smiling sadly. 'Johnny asked me to leave.'

'Johnny? Your Johnny asked you to leave?' Robin said. 'Now, wait a minute, I don't get this. This hunk of a guy, Johnny's friend, asks you to the dance. You go to the dance . . . By the way, you look great! I love that blue sweater. Can I borrow it sometime?'

Baby nodded her head and laughed as Robin continued her interrogation.

'OK, so you're at the dance. Now it's your turn. What *exactly* happened?'

Baby told how she'd arrived when the guys were singing and how she started to dance with Flash when Johnny cut in.

'He told me Flash wasn't used to going out with girls like me,' she blushed. 'I guess I'm too prissy or something, I don't know. He was exciting, but I was a little afraid of him too, for some reason. I don't know,' Baby said, sitting on her bed as she buttoned her nightgown and pulled up the covers.

'There was something wild about him that was both exciting and scary.

'Anyhow, Johnny asked me to go, so I left. That's really all there is to it. I went to see what was happening around the hotel and it's pretty quiet. So, here I am! Lucky you, Robin. I'm back!'

'Some story. And here I was imagining long sexy dances and sweet, heart-stopping kisses with this gorgeous hunk. I'm living vicariously, Baby. Your adventures are my adventures. Maybe I'll write a book about it someday,' she laughed.

'Well, tonight wasn't much of an adventure,' Baby observed. 'But it did leave me with an uneasy feeling. I told Johnny to say goodbye to Flash for me. I didn't even say goodbye.'

'Well,' Robin said, as she pulled on a nightgown and hopped into her bed, 'You'll probably see him again before he leaves.'

'Yeah, I guess so. But I still feel funny,' Baby said. 'Do you mind if we turn in early, Rob? This whole thing has given me a headache.'

'You know me,' Robin laughed. 'Two things I can always do – eat and sleep.'

She turned off the light. 'See you in the morning.'

Later that same night the door to Baby and Robin's room opened without warning.

Max peeked in, surprised to find the light turned off at 10.30. The squeaking door awakened the girls who sat up suddenly in their beds.

'Who's there?' Robin called out in terror.

'Girls, girls, it's me,' Max said, as he stood in the doorway and Robin turned on the light. 'I didn't think you'd be asleep,' he said. 'Hope I didn't scare you.'

'Uncle Max, what're you . . .' Robin trailed off as Max walked over to Baby's bed, sat down and took her hand.

'What's wrong, Dad?' she asked, her heart pounding, her face clouded with fear.

Max looked down and squeezed Baby's hand. 'I just got a call . . . They found a red Chevy . . . Jersey licence plates registered to Johnny . . .' He stopped, choked with emotion, floundering for words, unable to continue.

Baby stared at her father.

'What are you saying?'

'I don't know how many times I've told them to put a sign up at that damn turn,' he said, rubbing his eyes. 'Anyway, the car . . . skidded into the ravine. And he's uh . . . He . . . didn't make it, Baby.'

Baby stared at her father, unable to comprehend, as fear, stark and vivid, glittered in her eyes.

'Oh my God!' Robin sobbed, jumping over to Baby's bed and hugging her and Max. 'Oh, poor Johnny!'

Baby sat mute, her face like stone.

'I can't believe this. It can't be true,' she said in a far-a-way voice. 'Not Johnny. He just held me . . .' She trailed off, putting her head down on her pillow. Tears trickled from the corners of her eyes, as her father and Robin sat on her bed.

Baby awoke with a start.

'Robin?' she called, seeing her cousin's bed empty. 'Robin?'

She looked at the clock. 'Oh, it's 9.03! I missed my shift! It was that dream! That terrible dream!'

Baby lay back on the pillow staring at the cracked ceiling. She noticed the shape of a light bulb in one crack and what looked like a cereal bowl in another.

'What a terrible dream!' she repeated, recalling that her father had told her Johnny had been killed when his car went into a ravine.

Her head throbbed. 'I need an aspirin,' she said, as she walked to the bathroom. On the mirror was a note from Robin.

'Baby,' it read. 'Couldn't sleep after hearing about Johnny. See you later. Robin.'

Baby stared at the note in disbelief. She threw it to the floor, then picked it up and re-read it.

'About Johnny'? Could it be true?

Baby quickly pulled off her nightgown, pulled on some shorts and washed. She ran out of the cabin looking for Robin.

'It must be true,' she said to herself feeling a panic like she had never known well into her throat.

Suddenly she heard the sound of a ball hitting a wall. She looked up and her heart stopped. Johnny was playing handball, alone.

'Johnny!' she tried to shout, but no sound came out.

She ran to him, throwing her arms tightly around his neck 'Oh Johnny . . .' she cried.

Johnny hugged her back, then pushed her gently away and looked at her pale face and red puffy eyes.

'What's up?' he asked.

Baby stepped back, trying to register what she was seeing.

'Your car . . .' she said.

'So I gave it to him,' Johnny smiled. 'He deserved a break.' He bounced the ball. 'You know, I used to be just like him, 'cept I always thought there was something more. He never did. Maybe now he'll find it, find what's right for him.'

'You gave Flash your car?' Baby asked, her head swimming with a haze of confused emotions.

'Yeah, why?' he asked curiously now.

Baby reached out and pulled Johnny to her.

'Hold me,' she cried.

'What?'

'Just hold me. Tight,' she ordered, as Johnny looked down, perplexed and suddenly frightened.

Fifteen

The news of Flash's death hit Johnny like a thunderbolt.

'I should've gone with him. I had promised years ago,' he cried, slamming his fist onto his leg. 'If I was driving I would have known about the curve.'

Baby sat quietly opposite Johnny on a bench near the lake. He knew something was wrong when she had grabbed hold of him.

'Baby,' he had said. 'I like holding you. But what's wrong? Something must be wrong for you to be doing this now.'

The words stuck in her throat. Tears streamed down her puffy, red eyes as she told him what her father had said happened the night before.

At first Johnny stood in a trance. When she tried to reach out to him again, he screamed and pushed her away. He threw the hand ball hard against the backboard and ran over to it, banging his hands against the hot asphalt.

Baby was at a loss. She didn't know what to do. She stood and watched as Johnny worked through his initial shock pain and horror. He slid down the side of the backboard and sat, leaning against it for an hour, staring into space.

Finally, he stood up. 'I need to walk,' he said simply as he headed toward the lake. Baby followed him. They walked down the pathway, in between rocks, trees and bushes, until they found this bench, nestled at the edge of the beautiful mountain lake.

Johnny sat down. Baby followed. They sat in silence for another hour until, finally, Johnny started to talk, reminiscing about his youth, how he had met Flash in the schoolyard and telling all of the crazy pranks they had pulled over the years.

His laughter punctuated the stories but then the tears flowed. Baby reached over and held him. This time he didn't resist.

'Why couldn't it have been me!' he cried. 'It was my stupid car! He didn't even *ask* for it. I offered it. I gave him the keys, almost forced him to take them. I *killed him*!' he cried. '*Oh, Flash!* I'm so sorry!'

'You didn't kill him, Johnny,' Baby said gently. 'You know that. There are certain things over which we have no control things we can't predict, no matter what some stupid make-believe Swami who makes things up to entertain people says.'

Johnny listened and shrugged.

'I'll never forgive myself,' he said, choking on the words. 'He never had a chance. His old man kicked him out of his house. I don't even know if he'll bury him.'

'My father spoke to Flash's family, Johnny,' Baby said. 'All the arrangements are being taken care of. They were terrible to him but they still knew he was their son. It's so tragic when families only come together in death.'

'Some people don't even know family, real family,' Johnny said. 'Sometimes I think the kids here are more my family than my own.'

'They're *part* of your family, Johnny,' Baby said. 'But your mom and dad, you know how much they love you. And your brothers and sister too. They may be different, but they're still family.'

'Flash and I used to be like family,' Johnny sighed. 'I let him down, Baby. I sent him to follow his dream and now he's gone. I think my dreams died with him.'

'No, Johnny, No! You can't even think that. Flash wouldn't have wanted that. I spoke to him at the dance. He had a different understanding of dreams, but he believed in them too. And he would have wanted you to follow yours, to be the best dancer you could be. It would be a terrible waste to give that up because of your grief.'

'I don't think I can help myself, Baby,' Johnny cried. 'I feel like a part of me died with him.'

They sat for a while watching the water ripple on the lake as puffy white clouds bounced across a periwinkle blue sky.

Johnny took a deep breath and stood up. He reached his hand out to Baby.

'Thanks, Baby. I don't think there's anyone else in the world I could talk to like that but you. You're so special.'

He kissed her on the forehead and hand in hand they walked back up the hill from the lake.

Johnny's mourning lingered. He spent the rest of the day alone in his cabin, telling friends who stopped by, including Penny, that he just wanted to be alone.

The following morning Johnny heard a knock at the door.

'Who's there?' he called from his bed.

'It's me. Penny. Can I come in?'

He hesitated. 'Yeah, it's open.'

Penny walked in slowly. The room was dark. Clothing, records and magazines were tossed all over the floor. The place was a mess.

'Looks like a hurricane came through here,' Penny joked.

'No maid service today,' Johnny said dryly.

'Listen, Johnny, I'm worried about you. You can't lock yourself up in here. You've got a job to do and you've got to come back to the living.'

'I can't, Penny.'

'Listen,' she suggested, 'let's take a walk. I don't have lessons until after lunch. Let's just get out for a while.'

Johnny sighed.

'I'm gonna take a shower. I'll meet you in about an hour.'

'Great,' she smiled. 'I'll meet you outside.'

After showering and shaving Johnny at least looked better. He walked around with Penny until lunchtime talking about anything but the accident and Flash.

They strolled over to the main house and walked inside.

Outdoors, guests were eating lunch on the patio. The Swami Lou was again the featured entertainment and this time Robin was his star subject. Robin sat on the dais, her eyes closed, with a thick telephone book in her lap.

Swami Lou stood in front of her and issued his command. 'You will now open your eyes . . . and when I snap my fingers, you will perform the task I have assigned to you. All right, awaken!'

Robin opened her eyes. Suddenly, the Swami snapped his fingers. Robin picked up the phone book and tore it in half! She looked up at the Swami in amazement. The guests laughed and applauded. As they did, Penny and Johnny walked out of the dining room onto the patio.

Johnny's gaze was fixed and distant.

He looked around at the guests eating lunch, laughing, smiling, being entertained and he winced. 'You'd think something would . . . be . . . different. People would shut up a minute . . . something!' he cried.

'You want to get away from here?' Penny asked, taking his arm.

Johnny laughed bitterly. 'I shoulda done that two nights ago . . . with him.'

'You gotta stop saying that . . .' Penny begged.

'Right.'

'How about we go to work . . . take your mind off things?' Penny suggested.

Johnny stared at her in disbelief. 'Take my mind off *things*!' he almost shouted.

Penny took his hand and led him away from the patio. 'You know what I mean . . . come on.'

Later that afternoon, Johnny and Penny were in the rehearsal hall leading several kids in the routine to 'Night Train'.

The record played in the background. Penny, Jay, T.C., Cecily, Stephen and D.A. performed the routine Johnny had started when they first heard the song, days before.

Johnny paced back and forth as the kids danced, watching them anxiously. Stephen took a wrong turn and lost a beat.

'What're you deaf??' Johnny shrieked at him. 'Can't you hear that change?'

'Sorry,' Stephen said.

'Forget it,' Johnny answered harshly, pushing past him. The dancers stopped even though the music continued. Stephen looked at Johnny, hurt and embarrassed. Johnny ignored him and walked toward the record player. Penny walked over to Johnny.

'It's not working,' he said angrily.

'So make it work,' Penny challenged him.

'Come on, who are we kiddin'? I got a troupe of busboys and waiters here. You got a mechanic teaching you moves. What're we playing at? This isn't real! This isn't going anywhere!'

Penny ignored his outburst.

'Let's take it from the top,' she said.

'Leave me alone, OK?' Johnny said. 'Just get outta here!'

Penny's face dropped. 'OK. Sure. We'll take a break. No problem. Let's go,' she said to the kids, who followed her out the door.

Johnny stood very still after they left the hall. Then he started to dance. He heard the strains of the music in his head, but the room was silent. He started to perform the 'Night Train' routine, his expression unreadable, his face clenched and frozen.

He danced for several minutes, spinning and jumping, dipping and swirling when suddenly he held his hands to his ears. He heard the sound of screeching brakes and smashing metal. He tried to drown out the sound, overcome by the ferocity of his anger, frustration and sadness. His anguish welled up and suddenly he hurled himself against a wall, spinning off it, numbed to the pain. He rammed the wall again, trying to destroy his loss. At that instant, he saw his reflection in the far mirror. He turned away. He tried to return to the dance but felt himself losing all sense of himself once again.

Uncontrollably, he jumped on to a chair, breaking it with his weight. He turned and saw himself in the mirror, his eyes wild with rage and fear.

Finally, he grabbed a large copper vase and running into the mirror, hurled the vase straight at it, shattering the huge mirror with his tormented image staring back from the remaining pieces on the wall.

He slumped to the floor, weeping.

Sixteen

Johnny's rampage left the ballroom in a shambles.

Penny and the kids returned soon after Johnny's collapse and found him laying on the floor, bloody and asleep.

'Oh my God,' Penny cried, when she looked at Johnny and the room.

The kids quietly cleaned up around Johnny who remained asleep, all energy apparently spent from his frantic outburst.

'It's a good thing there's no show in here tonight,' Penny sighed, as she picked up the pieces of broken mirror. She looked at the huge wall of broken glass.

'More than seven years of bad luck here,' she sighed. The kids cleaned up what they could and left Johnny asleep.

Later that night, Max and a few guests sat on the patio chatting while Sweets played a soft tune on the piano.

'To the summer,' Max said, raising his glass in a toast to his guests, Mr and Mrs Zimmerman.

'May every one be as wonderful as this one,' Mrs Zimmerman smiled. They clinked glasses and sipped their drinks, enjoying the cool night air.

Suddenly, Johnny walked on to the patio, looking haggard and spent, his shirt torn, his forehead covered with dried blood.

'Can I talk to you, Mr Kellerman?' he asked Max.

Max looked at Johnny and gasped. 'Uh . . . certainly, Johnny,' he said, as he stood up and excused himself from the Zimmermans.

'We'll see you tomorrow, Max,' Mrs Zimmerman said.

The couple made a hasty exit, looking backward quickly at Johnny and Max.

Max looked at Johnny, bewildered and concerned.

'Have a seat?' he offered.

'No, thanks.'

'I hope you know how sorry I am about . . .' Max started.

'Yeah thanks. I appreciate your calling the family and all too. Baby told me about that. Look, Mr Kellerman. I uh, went a little . . . I kinda wrecked some stuff in the ballroom,' Johnny stammered.

Max took a deep breath, unsure how to react.

'Oh, well don't worry about it . . .'

'I'm gonna pay you back,' Johnny said.

'No need, Johnny. You've had a tough time.'

'I want to. I need to,' Johnny answered.

'OK,' Max nodded. 'Fine.'

Johnny shuffled as he felt a throbbing pain in his foot. 'Thing is . . . maybe you could give me some maintenance work or something,' he pleaded.

'I don't understand.'

Johnny looked down. 'I'm not going to dance anymore,' he said. Max stared at him at a loss for words. 'Penny can take over my place or you can find somebody . . .'

'Johnny, sit down a minute,' Max said gently, reaching out toward him.

But Johnny flinched away. 'Look, Mr Kellerman . . . It just doesn't make sense anymore. I thought it did, but . . . I don't know what I thought,' he stopped, holding back the tears, trying to hold himself together.

'Anyway, I'll do whatever work you give me to pay back the damage . . . then I'll be takin' off, OK?'

He turned to go. 'Johnny, wait,' Max called, but he was gone before Max could stop him.

The next morning, Johnny reported to the maintenance office early and was sent to put a new tether ball post into the playground.

He carried a shovel over his shoulder and marched to the playground. He marked out the site and started plunging the shovel into the earth with determined vehemence.

Penny walked by and stood watching. After a few minutes, she swallowed, tears streaming

down her face, and turned away from the
playground.

Johnny worked with ferocity, digging a hole,
sticking the tether ball pole into the hole and
measuring the hole's depth, before he started
digging again.

Nearby, Sweets sat on a swing, watching.

'What'cha doing this for Johnny?' Sweets asked,
causing Johnny to stop for a minute and look
up.

'I have to.'

'Penny said the old man doesn't care if you pay
him back or not,' Sweets said.

'*I* care. Why should I get special treatment?'
Johnny asked.

'You tryin' to make up for not bein' the one in
that car?' Sweets asked.

'Maybe if I'd been there we'd both be on the
road now, goin' somewhere . . . instead me bein'
stuck here in the same place . . . goin' nowhere
. . . and Flash . . .'

Johnny stuck the shovel deeper into the earth.

'I knew a guy once,' Sweets said. 'Nice guy,
but with a mean temper. Mean temper! Couldn't
keep his mouth shut. Anyway, he got into a thing
with some white guys in Philly. I was supposed
to meet him. Something held me up and I was
late. By the time I got there, they'd smashed
him up pretty bad. I kept thinkin' if only I got
there sooner, he would've made it. . . . But I
didn't.'

Sweets watched Johnny's expression. He didn't flinch.

'End of story, Johnny,' Sweets said. 'You gotta move on. Won't do no good otherwise.'

'The guy was my friend, man. We were part of the same thing. I came up with him,' Johnny said.

'That's true, Johnny. But you moved on. You're part of other people now . . . people here, who need you and count on you.'

'What people??' Johnny shouted. 'How do you make up for . . .' he stooped and looked down, biting his lip to keep under control. 'He was twenty-three, man! How do you move on after that? Where do you go?'

Johnny looked at Sweets for a minute, then lost control threw down his shovel and walked away.

Sweets sat on the swing, shaking his head.

'Poor kid. He's carrying that boy's body on his back, even now.'

Johnny walked quickly past the tennis courts where Penny was sitting on a bench. Baby and Robin walked up to the bench, dressed in tennis whites.

'How is he?' Baby asked Penny, as they watched Johnny hurry away.

'Not good,' Penny sighed.

Baby sat down opposite Penny. 'What are we going to do?' she asked.

Penny shook her head. 'I don't know,' she admitted.

Robin sat down next to Baby. 'There has to be something,' she said. 'there's *always* something!'

'What?' Penny asked, trying to be hopeful.

Robin shook her head. 'I don't know.'

The three young women sat in the warm sun staring at each other, trying to figure out someway to help ease Johnny's pain.

Baby turned to Penny. 'What if we made him believe in something . . . bigger than what happened?' she asked.

Penny looked confused. 'What do you mean?'

Baby turned to Robin. 'Tell her what you told me, about Swami Lou,' she asked Robin.

'Well, when I was being hypnotized by Swami Lou, which I think I was very brave to volunteer for in the first place . . .'

'Robin!' Baby glared. 'Get to the point.'

'OK, OK, well, at first I thought . . . God, is this guy a phoney, or what? But then, just before he hypnotized me, he said I had to surrender to something bigger than myself. And then, when he put me to sleep, it was like something *was* bigger than me . . . I mean, maybe I was just feeling light-headed cause I was hungry, but . . .'

Baby interrupted Robin and turned to Penny. 'What if we let him know how important he is . . . what he started . . . what he does. Convinced him how much he's needed . . . that everyone depends on him.'

'You think that would do it?' Penny asked, hopefully.

Baby shook her head. 'I think it's worth a try. We can't let him go on like this. My dad doesn't want him digging holes in the ground for tether ball. And that's not going to help him get through this,' she observed.

'So what do I say to him?' Penny asked, anxious to find a solution.

Baby smiled. 'You don't *say* anything.' She picked up her racket and stood up.

'Come on, girls,' Baby said. 'We've got work to do.' The trio walked hurriedly from the tennis courts chattering as they headed back to the main building.

Johnny finished installing the tether ball post. He reported back to the maintenance department.

'You know about wiring, Johnny?' the supervisor asked.

'Yeah,' Johnny said. 'I'm a mechanic in real life, remember?'

'That's what I heard. Though I think you're probably better as a dancer,' the supervisor smiled. 'Anyhow, I need someone to check out that wiring problem in the ballroom chandelier. Think you can handle it?'

'You got it,' Johnny said glumly, picking up a tool box and heading over to the ballroom rehearsal hall.

He stood atop a tall ladder to reach the fixture, and looked down on Penny and the dancers, who walked in to the hall, along with Baby.

No words were exchanged and Johnny quickly returned his attention to his work, avoiding their gaze.

Penny took a deep breath, forcing herself to keep from looking up the ladder at Johnny. She signaled to T.C., Stephen, Cecily, D.A., Paula, Andrea and Marceil to take their positions on the floor while Baby walked to the record player and put the needle on the 45 to 'Night Train'.

The dancers began the routine, making obvious mistakes, but sticking with it as they tried to imitate Penny.

Johnny stood atop the ladder for a moment, struggling with himself as he watched from the corner of his eye. Slowly he climbed down the ladder and headed for the door.

'It's not going to work,' he called angrily over the music as he headed toward the door. 'Your doing this isn't going to work. Don't you understand? I don't care. Get it? I don't care!'

'You gotta care, man,' D.A. called to Johnny.

Johnny stopped and turned toward the dancers. 'Look, I don't belong here, OK? Flash knew that. He knew me my whole life. He *knew* me!'

'He knew you *then*,' Penny said, brushing away a tear. 'We know you *now*.'

T.C. stepped out of the dance line. 'This is all about *you*, man! We don't cut it without you.'

Stephen stepped forward. 'If I'm not doin' this, I'm out stealing cars, for God's sake. You make the difference, man.'

Johnny tried to hold himself together, a look of tired sadness on his face.

'What about *him*?' he asked. 'What about Flash?'

'He wouldn't have wanted you to walk out on us,' Penny said.

'How do you know?'

'Because he loved you. Like us.'

Johnny looked at his friends, suddenly feeling a huge, painful knot inside. He shook his head and made it out the door before he broke down completely.

As he rounded the corner, just outside the rehearsal hall, he stopped and slumped down against the wall smothering a sob.

Johnny took a deep breath but the deep sobs racking the depths of his insides could not be contained. He wept aloud, rocking back and forth as he sat, his pain overwhelming him.

Inside the rehearsal hall, the dancers stood motionless, hearing the tormented pain of Johnny's cries.

Penny walked over to the record player to turn off the music.

Baby waved her away. 'Leave it on. Keep dancing,' she told Penny.

'What?'

'Do it!' Baby ordered.

Penny looked at her, helpless and confused, then signaled the kids back to dance.

As the music continued, Johnny reappeared in the doorway. He stared at them as they danced his inventive dance, moving to motions he had created to match the rhythm of the music.

The dancers continued to move, concentrating deeply to take the right steps, keep the right beat while stealing glances at Johnny, desperately willing him to like what he saw.

'You really think this means something? You really think that?' he called from the doorway as he slowly made he way inside, the music still playing, the dancers still moving.

'Talk to me!' he cried.

They continued to dance, struggling to remain focused on the work, undaunted by Johnny's presence.

Suddenly Stephen lost the beat, the same one he had lost in the last rehearsal. Johnny turned on him, almost unaware of what he was saying.

'Why can't you get that right?' he yelled. 'It's a simple goddamn move!'

The dancers heard Johnny and slowly stopped moving. Baby turned off the music. Stephen walked over to Johnny and stood in front of him.

He stood there for what seemed like a long time, a plea and a challenge in his eyes.

'Show me, man,' he asked.

The dancers stared at Johnny, waiting, unsure how he would react.

Johnny stared back at them and took a deep breath, pulling something up from within him, fighting to find the will to rally, to continue to live his own life.

The silence was deafening for what seemed endless minutes. Baby heard the clock tick once on the wall.

Then Johnny wiped the tears from his eyes and put his arm on Stephen's shoulder, leading him to the middle of the room.

'Cut the turn and try it from the break . . .' he said simply. 'And one and two and . . .'

He started Stephen dancing again, showing him the step, repeating the motions, calling out the directions. In a few minutes, Stephen got it right.

'Right! Right! You got it!' Johnny cried, as he fell in step and finished the routine with the others.

Tears streamed down Baby's face as she stood by the record player and watched Johnny come back to life. She saw the intensity and unity with which the group danced together and she cried, feeling both happy and sad. She slipped unnoticed out of the side door as the music and dancing continued.

'No matter how happy I feel for all of them,' she thought to herself, 'there's still a little part of me that feels so separate and alone. I wish I didn't feel like I was back at Roslyn High, like watching the kids come together when Dad read the list of those who were let go. I'm always the outsider looking in.

'I think I need a dose of Robin,' she sniffed, as she headed toward her cabin.

Seventeen

That night Baby lay in bed staring at the ceiling thinking about the past week.

The highs and lows of the last days played like a television re-run before her eyes: the horror of the hotel's financial problems and the solidarity of the staff members; Flash's sudden tragic death and Johnny's overwhelming grief.

Baby marveled as she lay, unable to close her eyes, let alone sleep, at how much her life had changed just by being at the hotel this summer. Even though her father, Robin and the kids provided a new kind of loving friendship she hadn't known before, she felt an inner longing for a real relationship that had not yet been satisfied. She knew that as much as she cared for Johnny, and often longed for him as well, they would not have a relationship now.

'Maybe someday?' she daydreamed, smiling. Her eyes were wide open. Too many thoughts, emotions, unsolved problems filled her head.

Robin lay in the other bed, apparently asleep.

'I wonder how she does it,' Baby asked herself. 'She's the best sleeper I've ever seen!'

Baby sighed, a deep, longing sigh and continued to stare.

'*What?*' Robin called with her eyes closed.

'What *what?*' Baby asked. 'I thought you were asleep.'

'How can anyone – even me – sleep with the moans coming from that bed!' her cousin asked.

'Baby,' Robin said, turning over and facing her cousin, her eyes now open and her mouth going as usual. 'You sound like a steam leak. And it's ninety-five degrees outside! Is this a "my life is over and you should get up and talk to me, Robin", sigh? Or a "boy am I depressed but go ahead and sleep anyway" sigh? Come on. Which is it? I haven't got all night. I need my beauty sleep, you know.'

Baby sat up and looked over at her cousin, whose head was filled with huge curlers, her face covered with cream.

'There's only one Robin,' she thought to herself. She smiled. 'I'm glad you're here, Robin. I just want you to know that.'

'OK, enough with the compliments. What's the story?'

Baby sighed again.

'There it is, the steam leak. Let's go, Baby. What's on your mind? This is Dr Robin, here, ready to answer your every question.'

'Did you ever feel like you'd never fit in anywhere?' Baby asked sullenly. 'That nobody cares if you live or die? That you're all alone and this is the best it'll ever get?'

Robin nodded emphatically. 'Almost every day.'

Baby looked astonished. 'Really? What do you do?'

'Eat.'

'Good idea.' Baby looked around. 'What do we have?'

'Nothing. I ate it all.'

'Robin, I'm serious!' baby said. 'This business with Johnny and Flash, it made me feel well, sad and pensive, a part of things and an outsider, all at once. I had the most wonderful talks with Johnny. He told me he couldn't talk to anyone the way he could talk to me. But even so, I wasn't really the one who was able to help him through his pain.

'And Flash's death. I never had to deal with a young friend dying before. I danced with him. I know he liked me. But I left without ever saying goodbye. The thought of losing someone like that . . . it's more than I can bear. I feel like I've really grown up a lot this week. Can it have been just this week? With the hotel nearly going down the tubes and the kids rallying together so they could all stay. And then Flash and the car crash. I feel like it's too much to handle. Anyhow, I guess all this emotional stuff made me feel lonely. But most of all, it made me feel like I'm missing something, someone, in my own life.'

'OK, you want serious, I can see that now,' Robin said. 'Fine. The sun will come up tomorrow. You will laugh again. Somewhere out there are men for both of us. And most important of all . . . are you listening, Baby?'

'Yes.'

'Most important, either shut up and let me sleep or go get us some Twinkies.'

'I'm not hungry now,' Baby said.

'Great,' Robin growled. 'I wasn't either until you started talking about food!'

'I just want . . . somebody,' Baby sighed again. 'Is that too much to ask?'

'Not as far as I'm concerned,' Robin said. 'Be patient. You'll find him. Believe me, I've been to the outer limits with the Swami,' she said knowingly. 'I know these things.'

Baby laughed. 'Robin, you're too much! Thanks. G'night!'

Robin rolled back on her side and was soon fast asleep. But Baby's restlessness kept her awake.

She heard the humming of Robin's snoring fill the cabin.

Still she couldn't sleep. Baby pushed off the covers and pulled on her bathrobe and slippers. She quietly pushed open the screen door and walked out on to the porch. It was a cool, starry night, the feeling of summer creeping into the air.

She gazed up at the sky, which twinkled full of bright stars under a beautiful moon.

'What a glorious night,' she thought. 'In spite of everything, it makes you glad to be alive.'

And suddenly she knew. Knew Robin was right. Everything *would* work out all right, as long as she had the courage to face up to the future, follow her own dream - just like Johnny was now following his again.

Don't miss . . .

Book Six

OUR DAY WILL COME

Turn over the page for a sneak preview

OUR DAY WILL COME

If you had asked Max Kellerman what the first thought was that came into Johnny Castle's mind each morning, Max would have said one of three things: food, cars, or girls. 'Boys like that,' Max would have said, 'what else do you think they think about all the time? It's either their stomachs, their Chevys, or their, you know, their hormones.'

But the truth was that, for the past few days at least, the first thought that had come into Johnny's mind when he woke up was the same as the last thing he thought about as he fell asleep: Jack Benny. Well, not Jack Benny exactly. What had been preoccupying Johnny was the new routine he was working on to perform the weekend Benny came up to Kellerman's. It had to be special, really special. He wanted to make Max notice just how good he and the other dancers were. How professional, how imaginative, how innovative. He wanted people to remember the night not just because Jack Benny had told a few jokes he or someone else had probably told a hundred times before, but because Johnny Castle had done the choreography.

This morning, however, Johnny opened his eyes just as dawn broke over the Catskills, dance steps and famous comedians far from his thoughts. He leaned over to check the time on the alarm clock, then fell back against the pillow with a sigh. Sweets. Sweets and Martine. He closed his eyes. He'd had this crazy dream. It had been straight out of *West Side Story*, and yet it had seemed so real. His heart was still pounding.

The dream had taken place in a school yard. In the center of the yard there was a house. It was an average, ordinary sort of house, with a front porch and a garage and a driveway. It had a television antenna on the roof and a bird feeder out front. It looked nice. Like a real family lived in it. He remembered thinking, that's a nice house, I wouldn't mind living there. There was an electric mower and a kid's bike on the lawn. And he could see into the house. It was that kind of dream. He could see the living room and the kitchen and the bedrooms. He could see the magazines on the coffee table and the jar of peanut butter and the used knife on the formica counter near the sink. The only unusual thing about the house was that it was sitting in the middle of a basketball court. And that on either side of the house, at different ends of the school yard, were two gangs. The Sharks and the Jets. The Sharks were surrounding Sweets. The Jets were surrounding Martine. Music was playing. Sweets and Martine were trying to get to the house. It was their house. And if they could get to the house they'd be safe. They'd be together. Everything would be all right. But the gangs wouldn't let them get to the house. Every time they took a step forward someone yanked them back. Or blocked their way. Or waved a knife in their faces.

'Why are you doing this to them?' Johnny
wanted to yell. But it was a dream and no one could
hear him. The music got louder and louder. Sweets
was bleeding from the lip. Martine was struggling
against these guys who were holding her. She was
calling to Sweets. He was punching wildly, but he
was more than outmatched. Martine broke free
and started running towards the house. The door
was open. She was screaming his name. He was
fighting his way nearer and nearer to the house.
The music changed. It was Ben E. King singing
'Stand By Me'. And suddenly, instead of Martine
running towards the house, it was Baby. 'Johnny!'
she was shouting. 'Johnny! Johnny! You've got
to try! You can't give up!' And she was right, it
wasn't Sweets at all getting the crap kicked out
of him by the Sharks. It was him. 'Johnny!' Baby
screamed as she jumped on to the porch. 'Johnny!
Run! Run!'

Safe in his bed, with the alarm clock ticking
and the early light slipping in under the blinds,
Johnny opened his eyes again. And wondered
what Sweets and Martine were going to do.

Sweets glanced up as the kitchen door opened
and Johnny walked in. He reached for another
cup. 'You're up early, man,' he said over his
shoulder.

'Me?' Johnny watched Sweets' hand shake
as he poured out two cups of fresh coffee. He
looked about ten times worse than Johnny felt.
'I thought it was against your religion to get up
before lunch time.'

Sweets smiled. It was a smile as false as
Johnny's grandmother's teeth. 'Yeah, well . . .' he
mumbled, 'I couldn't sleep. You know, too hot.'

Johnny nodded. 'Yeah, I know. I couldn't sleep either.'

Sweets picked up his cup. 'What say we take these out on the verandah? Catch the last of the sunrise.'

'So,' said Johnny, once they were both leaning against the rail, looking out towards the mountains where the sky was still tinged with gold.

'So,' said Sweets.

'Looks like we're in for another scorcher,' said Johnny.

Sweets nodded. 'Yeah, it sure does.'

'It must be murder in the city,' said Johnny.

'Yeah,' agreed Sweets, 'it must be murder.'

Johnny tapped his foot. The birds chirped and chattered. Sweets kept his eyes fixed on the distance.

'So you couldn't sleep either, huh?' said Johnny.

'No,' said Sweets.

Johnny looked over at him. He had seen Sweets after an all-night jam. And he'd seen him after a night of celebrating a Yankees' victory. But hadn't ever seen him look this rough. Where Johnny came from, you didn't talk much about personal problems. Women did. Women were always getting involved in everybody else's lives, but not men. Men kept to themselves. If a buddy of yours had a bad time – if he'd just gotten drafted or his girlfriend had left him or something like that – you might take him out for a couple of beers, but you wouldn't expect him to say a lot. You wouldn't expect him to tell you how he really really felt. Johnny turned back to the mountains, looking brand-new in the morning sunshine. Where he came from was what he was trying to escape, wasn't it? He took a deep breath. 'You wanna talk about it?' he asked in a rush.

Sweets didn't blink. 'Talk about what?'

Johnny shrugged. 'You know . . .'

Sweets leaned forward. 'Yeah, I know. What I don't know is how you know.'

'Well, we were all there last night . . . I mean, it doesn't take much to put one and one together and—'

'You've been talkin' to Baby, right?' He didn't wait for Johnny to reply but went on. 'The trouble with Baby is she thinks everything's possible in this world. But you and me,' said Sweets, glancing over at the young man staring into his empty coffee cup, 'you and me, we know that's not true.'

'Yeah,' agreed Johnny, 'we know that . . . but—'

'There ain't no buts,' said Sweets quickly. 'Let me tell you a little story, okay? It's about this young colored guy, right? Now this guy is an ace musician. He can play the guitar. He can play the piano. He plays, he writes, he arranges. He's not the best, maybe, but he's real real good. Only thing he needs is a chance, right? Just one chance. And this audition comes up for this very famous band. They're goin' on a nationwide tour and they're lookin' for a new piano player. Our colored kid, he's been playing clubs and bars since he was old enough to get in the door, and he knows he's hot.' He paused for a second, watching the sky. 'You know what I mean, Johnno? Really hot.'

Johnny nodded, not looking around.

'So he goes to this audition. He pushes his way in and he gets a hearing and he's terrific. But he doesn't get the job. He doesn't get the job because this band is not about to go on a nationwide tour with a colored piano player. What happens when they get to Atlanta? Or even Minneapolis? What happens when they want to go in for a meal or get a hotel for the night?'

'Yeah, but Sweets, that was a while ago. Things are changin'—'

'They're not changin' that much. I had the talent for that job, Johnny, but I couldn't have it because I wasn't the right color. I would've caused too much trouble. And as far as I can see, Martine's just like that job.'

'Yeah, but Sweets, maybe if—'

'And y'know what else? I wonder a lot what would've happened if they'd offered me that job. If I'd really thought about everything that was involved, would I've taken it? And if I had, then what? How long before it got too much for me? Or too much for the rest of the band? How long before they started hatin' me and I started hatin' them?'

'But if they'd really wanted you . . . if they'd been willin' to take the risks . . .'

Sweets stood up straight. 'I don't wanna talk about it any more.'

Johnny was looking at the beautiful Kellerman's view, the view families came back for year after year, but what he was seeing was that stupid dream. Martine running for the house. Baby shouting to him.

'Look, Sweets,' he said, groping for the right words, 'I know this is none of my business—'

'You said it,' said Sweets. 'It's none of your business.'

Johnny tried again. 'Yeah, well, it's not like I'm trying to interfere or anything.'

Sweets was starting to walk away. 'Then don't.'

Johnny swung around in exasperation. 'Will you at least give me a chance to say what I wanna say? I mean, you've talked me through one or two things, and I've appreciated that.'

Sweets stopped in the doorway. 'And I appreciate what you're tryin' to do, really, but, believe me, Johnny, this is different.'

Johnny, the morning behind him, watched Sweets walk into the darkness of the hotel. One of the voices in his head was saying, 'Sweets is right. It is different.' But another voice, one that sounded suspiciously like Frances Kellerman, was saying, 'What are you talking about, "different"? It's all part of the same life, isn't it?'

'Robin,' Baby was saying as they walked past the shady grove where Penny was teaching an eager group of middle-aged couples how to do the hokey-pokey and towards the pool, 'I thought you promised you wouldn't tell anybody about Sweets and Martine.'

'I didn't,' said Robin, looking shocked. 'Who would I tell?'

'Well, I don't know,' said Baby, 'but it's not even time for lunch and half the staff seems to know.'

Robin came to a sudden stop and put her hands on her hips. 'Who, Baby? You have to substantiate your allegations. Who knows?'

Baby held up one hand and started ticking names off on her fingers. 'Norman.'

'Oh, Norman,' Robin waved the name away. 'I just happened to run into him on my way to calisthenics. He brought it up first, Baby. Really. I told him my lips were sealed, but he forced it

Baby seemed unconvinced. 'Oh, sure, Norman Bryant, the Russians' secret weapon. The KGB uses him when they have spies they can't make talk.'

'Really, Baby. You know how persistent Norman can be.'

'Sherry.'

Robin looked over towards the hokey-pokeyers. They were shaking it to the left, and shaking it to the right, seeming to be having the time of their lives. She wished, all of a sudden, that she was lined up with them, and not standing here being grilled by Baby. 'Sherry? Well, Sherry brought me my breakfast, and you know how it is. One minute you're talking about the eggs and the next minute—'

'Penny.'

'Penny?'

'Yeah, Penny. You remember Penny. Did she bring you your breakfast, too?'

'Nooo. She came over to me while I was doing my deep knee-bends. You know what a bully she is, Baby. It's because she grew up on the streets. I wouldn't be surprised if she owns a knife. And anyway, she wouldn't leave me alone until I'd told her everything I knew.'

'Andy.'

Robin held up her hands. 'Oh, no, Frances Kellerman, you can't get me for Andy. He must've overheard me talking to Arlene—'

'Arlene? You even told the chambermaid?'

'Well, I—'

'Oh, Robin, what am I going to do with you?' Baby wondered why she even bothered getting upset. She'd known this was going to happen. She should probably be grateful that she hadn't woken up to Robin telling the story of Sweets and Martine over the PA system.

'I don't know what you're getting so upset about,' said Robin, in the same tone she'd used when she had the little accident last spring with her father's car. 'Everybody's very sympathetic.' This news seemed to make Baby feel as good as the information that the other car looked worse than theirs had made her father feel.

'Oh, great!' Baby threw her hands in the air. 'Well, everything's all right then. Maybe you could arrange to have everybody sing "Somewhere" after supper. That should cheer Sweets up.'

'I don't know what you're getting so sarcastic about, Baby,' said Robin.

'You're the one who wanted to help Martine. Surely getting everybody on her side is one way of doing that. If Sweets sees that they've got support—'

Baby held up her hand. 'Wait a minute, Robin. I thought you were the one who said I shouldn't interfere. I thought you were the one who said Sweets being colored and Martine being white wasn't a little difference you could overlook.'

'What can I say?' asked Robin with a shrug. 'I dreamed about *West Side Story* all night long. And anyway,' she grinned, 'you know I've always been a hopeless romantic.'

We hope you enjoyed reading this book. If you would like to receive further information about available titles in the Bantam series, just write to the address below, with your name and address: Kim Prior, Bantam Books, 61–63 Uxbridge Road, Ealing, London W5 5SA.

If you live in Australia or New Zealand and would like more information about the series, please write to:

Sally Porter
Transworld Publishers
(Australia) Pty Ltd
15–23 Helles Avenue
Moorebank
NSW 2170
AUSTRALIA

Kiri Martin
Transworld Publishers (NZ) Ltd
Cnr. Moselle and
Waipareira Avenues
Henderson
Auckland
NEW ZEALAND

All Bantam and Young Adult books are available at your bookshop or newsagent, or can be ordered at the following address: Corgi/Bantam Books, Cash Sales Department, PO Box 11, Falmouth, Cornwall, TR10 9EN.

Please list the title(s) you would like, and send together with a cheque or postal order. You should allow for the cost of book(s) plus postage and packing charges as follows: 60p for the first book, 25p for the second book and 15p per copy for each additional book, to a maximum of £1.90.

Please note that payment must be made in pounds sterling; other currencies are unacceptable.

(The above applies to readers in the UK and the Republic of Ireland only)

BFPO customers, please allow for the cost of the book(s) plus the following for postage and packing: 60p for the first book, 25p for the second book and 15p per copy for the next 7 books, thereafter 9p per book.

Overseas customers, please allow £1.25 for postage and packing for the first book, 75p for the second book, and 28p for each subsequent title ordered.

It's hot! It's sexy! It's fun!

Baby's life changes forever when she meets Johnny. For
he is an electrifying dancer, and he shows Baby what
dancing is *really* all about – the heat, the rhythm and the
excitement . . .

A sensational series based on the characters from the
top-grossing *Dirty Dancing* movie and television series.

Available now:

1. BABY, IT'S YOU
2. HELLO, STRANGER
3. SAVE THE LAST DANCE FOR ME
4. BREAKING UP IS HARD TO DO
5. STAND BY ME
6. OUR DAY WILL COME